Rhoda Broughton

Good-Bye Sweetheart!

Volume 3

Rhoda Broughton

Good-Bye Sweetheart!
Volume 3

ISBN/EAN: 9783337348038

Printed in Europe, USA, Canada, Australia, Japan

Cover: Foto ©Andreas Hilbeck / pixelio.de

More available books at **www.hansebooks.com**

A Tale.

BY

l.i   · ·

AUTHOR OF

"COMETH UP AS A FLOWER," AND "RED AS A ROSE IS SHE."

IN THREE VOLUMES.

VOL. III.

LONDON:

RICHARD BENTLEY AND SON.

1872.

CONTENTS OF VOL. III.

PART II.—*continued.*

PART III.

NIGHT.

"GOOD-BYE, SWEETHEART!"

PART II.—*continued.*

CHAPTER XIV.

WHAT JEMIMA SAYS.

R. SCROPE returns to the drawing-room, as he left it, alone.
As he enters, we both look up
and smile, as one does smile with vague
complacency at the sight of anything
young and specially comely.

" Did you find her ?" I ask, as I kneel
before the fire, giving it a vigorous and
searching poke, for his benefit.

" Yes."

He says merely this almost the shortest
of all monosyllables but there is something in the tone in which he says it that
makes me pause, pen in hand, from my
noisy toil, to examine him more narrowly.

" You have been quarrelling, as usual,
I suppose ?" I say, with a wily attempt to
come at the matter of their conversation
without seeming too overtly curious.

" Lenore always quarrels with everybody," says Sylvia, pouring the pug's fat
stomach, as he lies on his back, with his
eyes rolling awfully and a bit of rosy
tongue showing between his black lips, in
a state of Sybaritic enjoyment on her lap.
" I tell her it is her own flirting. She
always maintains that she cannot flirt—
does not know how ; of course that is
nonsense, I suppose we all do a little
in that way, if we —holding her
smooth head rather aside, and looking arch.

" Has she been saying anything un-usually exasperating ?" I ask, as, under my successful labours, the frosty fire spires and races upwards. " Never mind if she has ; she is not in very good tune just now, poor soul, and one can hardly wonder at it."

While he speaks, Mr. Scrope has been stalking up and down in a fidgety way, making the boards creak. At my words he stops, and says abruptly, " Why ?"

" Have not you heard ? Oh, of course not ! Stupid of me ! She would not be likely to mention it herself—it is not a very pleasant subject to talk about—but her engagement is all off, and she is natur-ally rather low about it."

" She is not in the least low; I never saw her in better spirits in my life," says Scrope, with a brusqueness that amounts to incivility ; and having delivered himself of this speech, he marches off to the window and turns his back to us.

" It must be *your* coming, then, that has cheered her," says Sylvia, laughing lackadaisically; "and indeed to tell you the truth, at the risk of making you atrociously conceited, I must say *I don't wonder at it.* It is a shockingly fast sentiment, I suppose, but there is something in the *timbre* of a man's voice that quite invigorates me; I suppose it is always having been so much used to men's society. I get on with them so much better than with women; *I* understand *them*, and *they* understand *me*."

" Have you had any talk with her?" I ask, rising precipitately, and following him to the embrasure of the window, perfectly heedless of the fact that my sister is comfortably mounted on her pet hobby—*self*, and is cantering complacently away on him. " Did she say anything to you?"

" Listen !" he says, putting a hand on each of my shoulders, quite unconscious of the familiarity of the action—and indeed they might be posts for all he knows about them—and looking me redly and triumphantly in the face. " She has been saying *this* to me : ' I will marry you as soon as you like !' "

" WHAT ! ! ! ! ! !" Six marks of admiration but poorly render the expression I throw into this innocent monosyllable. I feel my face becoming a series of round *Os*—astonishment stretching and opening every feature beyond its natural destiny.

" Why do you keep staring at me ?" says the young man, petulantly, giving me a little shake; "why do you stand with your mouth wide open ? Why should not I marry ? What is there to prevent me ? Does not everybody do it? What is there so very surprising in it ?"

Still I maintain an absolute silence ; his

hands have dropped from my shoulders,
but I still stand before him, like a block of
stupid stone.   Neither does Sylvia speak ;
she is affecting to blow her nose, and has
covered the more part of her face with her
pocket-handkerchief ; what yet remains is
excessively red.   For once her hobby-
horse has given her a nasty fall.

"Why do you stare at me like a wild
beast ?" cries Scrope angrily.   " Is this
the way you always take a piece of news?
Pleasant for the person who tells you, if it
is.   If I had told you that she had just
fallen down dead in the next room you
could not look at me with greater dis-
may."

I cannot contradict it.   Sputtering and
breathless, I still face him, trying hard to
speak ; but in all the wide range of good,
noble, and useful words that the English
tongue affords, I can find not one that
suits the present crisis.

" Why don't you say *something ?*" says the young man, with cheeks on fire and lightning eye. " The most disagreeable sentence you could invent would be better than this. Oh, come! I cannot stand it any longer—to be stared at by two per- fectly silent women with their mouths open ; it would make"—laughing fiercely —" it would make the bravest man in Europe run like a hare !"

He turns quickly to the door as he speaks. Then I find my tongue ; its hinges are not well oiled, and it does not run smoothly, but it goes somehow. I catch hold of his arm or his coat tail—I am not quite sure which, in my excitement. ·" Stop, stop !" I cry, incoherently ; " don't be cross !—I mean to say something—I am going to say something—but—but—you take my breath away ! It is so *sudden*—so *unnaturally* sudden !"

" *Unnaturally ?*" repeats he, tartly ; the

painful consciousness that I have hit upon
the joints of his harness making him de-
fend the weak part with all the greater
acrimony. " Why *unnaturally*, pray ? If
it does not seem too sudden to her or to
me, I do not see why it need appear so to
any one else."

" But—but—are you *sure* you are not
mistaken ?" I say, disbelievingly, mindful
of the tear-swollen desperate face I had
seen lying among its tossed hair on my
sister's bed-room floor ; " are you quite
sure she said those words ? She is an odd
girl—Lenore—very odd, and sometimes
she has a random way of talking ; I do not
think she quite knows always what she is
saying."

" Thank you," replies he, bowing, form-
ally, though his face flames. " You are—
if not polite—at least candid. I understand. A woman must be slightly de-
ranged to consent to be my wife ?"

My wits are still too far out wool-gathering for me to be able to summon them back to compose some civil explanation and apology.

"You disbelieve me still?" cries my future brother-in-law, greatly exasperated by my silence. "All right! do—it does me no harm; but if it should happen to strike you at any time that I may, *by accident*, be speaking truth, you have only to send for Lenore, and ask her."

"Poor dear Lenore!" says Sylvia, speaking for the first time, and smiling, sweetly. "She has not been long in consoling herself, has she? I am *quite* glad."

Mrs. Prodgers has finished blowing her nose, and her face has laid aside its transient redness, but she now holds her head quite straight, nor does she look at all arch. "You know, Jemima, if you remember, you laughed at me—but I always maintained that Paul Le Mesurier did not

care two straws about her.   I am sure I am
the last person to pretend to unusual clear-
sightedness, but one has one's instincts !"

" It *is* sudden, of course !" burst out
Scrope, boyishly, not paying any attention
to my sister, but looking straight and defiantly at me.   " What is the good of tell-
me that ?   How can I help it ?   Tell me
that January is colder than July—I know
it is ; but it is not my fault.   If I had had
my way it would not have been sudden—it
would have happened full six months ago.
No one ought to know that better than
you."

" Ought I ?" say I vaguely.   " I dare
say—but to tell you the truth—so many
incoherences about Lenore—her eyes, her
ankles, and her inhumanities—have been
poured into my ears, that I get them mud-
dled together ; I cannot, at a moment's
notice, assign to each lover his own several
Jeremiad."

"You are spiteful," replies the young fellow, laughing a little, but looking offended. "If I had known how little you were listening to me I would not have talked to you about her."

"Poorest, dearest Lenore!" repeats Sylvia, smiling a little patronisingly. "Quite the dearest thing in the world, and, mercifully for her, incapable of fretting much about anything or anybody. What a gift!—if she could but give one the receipt"—sighing and pensively passing through her fingers the beads of a great jet rope, that she wears round her neck.

"Jemima!" says Scrope, impulsively, putting his hand again fraternally on my shoulder. "I do not suppose that they will do me any good—not a barleycorn ; but still I have a morbid desire for your good wishes; they will be tardy and lugubrious, I am aware, but such as they are,

give them me.   If *I*" (reproachfully) " had
heard that *you* were going to be married I
should not have been so slow or so dismal
in offering mine."

" That is a very safe position," reply I,
drily; " if you had seen me flying towards
the moon you would have complimented
me on the ease and grace with which I
flapped my wings.   I *do* wish you good
luck—there !—but whether you will *get* it
or not is another matter."

" But—but—you—think that it *will*
be ?" says Scrope, with his whole eager
heart in his voice.   " Now that you have
shut your mouth, and that your eyes no
longer look as if they were falling out of
your head, and that you can talk rationally
—you *believe* it ?"

" Upon my honour I cannot say," reply
I, laughing uncomfortably, " Lenore, as
Sylvia truly observed just now, is quite the
dearest thing in the world, but sometimes

she goes round and round, like the sails of a windmill. I have a good mind to go and ask her myself." So I go.

CHAPTER XV.

WHAT JEMIMA SAYS.

"UP and down, up and down, up and down, with her hands behind her back, I find her marching in the ordered solitude of her own room, as I had expected.

"Good heavens!" say I, entering, with my shoulders raised nearly to my ears, and my hands spread out.

She stops in her persevering trudge, looks me coolly over, and says,

"*Après ?*"

I throw my eyes up to the ceiling, and

shake my head several times, but words utter I none.

"You have heard, I suppose," she says quietly. "I see he is running all over the house *button-holing* everybody, as the Ancient Mariner did the Wedding Guest. I hope he has told Morris, and William, and Frederic—it would be a sad oversight if he has not."

"It *is* true, then?" I say, gasping. "When he told me I would not believe it —I said so—I said I would ask you myself."

"You might have saved yourself the trouble of the journey upstairs," replies she, calmly, "but as you are not 'fat and scant of breath,' like Hamlet, Prince of Denmark, I suppose it does not matter much."

"*Good* heavens!" say I, for the second time.

"Try a new ejaculation," suggests my sister, smiling; "I am tired of that one."

" And—and—and your *reason* ?"

" *Reason* ?" repeats she, laughing rather harshly. " What extraordinary questions you do ask ! Is not it on the surface ? I am *in love*, to be sure—deeply in love."

I am on the verge of being delivered of a third, " Good heavens !" but, recollecting myself, suppress it.

" If you remember, you did not approve of my first choice," says Lenore, with a bitter smile ; "are you any better pleased with my second ?"

" *Much* better," I answer emphatically ; "far better—only it is horribly and *indecently* sudden—that is all !"

Silence.

" As for the other," I continue, " you are right. I never *could* understand what you saw in him : a long nose, a yard of scarlet beard, and a sulky temper, seemed to me his whole stock-in-trade."

For one second her eyes flash with a furious pain, then grow quiet.

" Exactly," she says, composedly. " Now in the case of the *present* nose there is nothing to be desired, is there ?—nice and short, and runs straight down the middle of his face, without deviating a hair's breadth to right or left ; such *nice* curls, too, all over his head, as if they were put in curl papers every night—and such *dear* little teeth !"

" For shame !" cry I, indignantly ; " you are describing a *doll*. Lenore ! Lenore ! what are you made of ? Beauty and love are thrown away upon you, and you have a perverted taste for ugliness and indifference."

She shrugs her shoulders.

" One may abuse one's own property, I suppose. If you remember he is *my* doll now—curls and dear little teeth and all !"

I turn away, pained and disgusted.

"Stay," she says, laying her hand on mine ; "do not be cross.   I am serious— look at me !   I am sure I do not feel as if there were a joke to be got out of the whole of me."

I look at her, as she tells me—look with uncomfortable misgivings at the bright beauty that has prospered her so little : her cheeks are crimson, and the hand which holds mine burns, *burns*.

" Attend to me," she says imploringly. " I am *very* much in earnest.   I have done better *this* time, have not I ?   I have been more wise at last ?"

I shake my head.   " How can I say ?"

" This one is much more suitable to me, is not he ?   I—I " (laughing feverishly) " I begin to think that I did not care *really* for the other so much after all ; it was only *fancy* — it was only my perversity.   I wanted to get him because I thought nobody else could. I—I was not *really* fond of him, was I ?"

She looks with a sort of wild wistfulness into my face for confirmation of her words, but I do not think she finds any.

" He is much more suitable to me," she repeats vaguely, as if trying to convince herself by iteration ; " much more in every respect. So much better-looking."

"Immeasurably," say I emphatically ; " not that I see what *that* has got to say to it."

"And better off," she continues, still holding and unconsciously pressing my hand with her hot dry fingers. "We should have been miserably poor, Paul and I—*miserably ;* and I hate poverty ; I hate trying to make both ends meet. They will meet now and *lap* over without any difficulty, will not they ?"

" I imagine so."

" And in age, too," she goes on eagerly,

"we are far better fitted; is it not so? Paul was old—older than his age even— old in himself."

" He might well have been your father," I say, laughing vindictively, "except that no one would have accused you of emanating from so hard-featured a stock."

" No," she says, not in the least attending to my sarcasm, "of course not; altogether, you see," smiling mechanically— "altogether you see, Jemima, it is all for the best. I am *nearly quite* convinced of it now, and of course I shall grow more and more convinced every day, shall not I ?"—looking at me with imploring inquiry.

I make no response, and we both lapse into silence—a silence spent by Lenore in wandering aimlessly about, pulling the blinds up and down, disarranging the few wintry flowers in the vase on the toilet table, altering the furniture. At last she speaks with sudden abruptness :

" It is to be soon—very soon !"

" He is wise there, I think," I answer, following her doubtfully about with my eyes. " Poor boy, he has not studied you for the last six months to no purpose ; he knows what a weathercock you are, and is bent on making sure of you while you are in the vein. Who can tell when the wind may change ?"

" You are mistaken," she says, quickly, " it was not *his* idea at all ; it was *my* suggestion. I suppose " (laughing with the same forced and hollow sound that had before pained me)—" I suppose it is the first instance on record of such a proposition emanating from the lady, but it was. Yes, you may look as if you were going to eat me—I cannot help that—it *was !*"

" Good heavens !" repeat I, devoutly, lapsing unintentionally, for the third time, into my favourite ejaculation.

" Yes, soon—very soon !" she says, half

to herself, pulling her rings on and off, lacing her fingers together and then again unlacing them ; "and we will have a very smart wedding—very! I hate sneaking to church with only the clerk and the beadle, as if one were ashamed of oneself. We will have all the neighbours, and men down from Gunter's, and a ball."

I stare distrustfully at her : her eyes are sparkling like diamonds at night, the splendid carnation that fever gives paints her cheeks.

"And you will have it put in *all* the papers," she says, laughing restlessly ; "*all* of them—you must not forget—a fine long flourishing paragraph—do you mind ?—in *all* of them."

"What an extraordinary thing to give a thought to !" I say, suspiciously. "If you had two columns of the *Times* devoted to you, how much good would it do you ?"

"*Good?* Oh, none at all; but it is

amusing. Flowers of newspaper elo-
quence are always entertaining, don't you
know ? And one likes one's friends—one's
friends at a distance—to know what is
happening to one."

A light begins to break upon me, but it
is such an unpleasant one that for the
moment I ask no more questions. A
pause. There are so many things—true,
yet eminently disagreeable—to be said,
that I hesitate which to begin upon.
Lenore presently saves me the trouble.

" If—if—he were to see me now," she
says, sitting down at my feet, and smiling
excitedly up at me, " he could not think I
was pining much for him, could he ?"

The unpleasant light grows clearer.

" When he sees the account of my wedding in the papers—so soon—so immediately—such a brilliant marriage, too ; I
am so glad it is a good one—he will
realise " (laughing ironically) " how irre-

parable an injury his desertion has inflicted
on me, will not he ?"

" *Is it possible ?* " say I, with shocked
emphasis.   " I   suspected   it   when   you
began to talk to me ; I am *sure* of it now.
Lenore ! Lenore ! you are going to be
madder than all Bedlam and Hanwell
together !"

" I am—am I ?" speaking with listless
inattention to my words, and still pursuing
her own thoughts.

" Marrying one man to pique another
always seemed to me the most thorough
' pulling your nose to vex your face,' " I
continue, in great heat.

No remark, no comment on my homely
illustration.

" Suppose he does hear of your marriage ; suppose he does read every paragraph in all the papers about it ; suppose
he reads that you had twelve bridesmaids,
and that you went off in a coach-and-six,

how much the worse will he be, or how much the better you ?"

Still no answer; but she listens.

" He will feel a little stab of pain, per-haps—of mortified vanity, more likely; but it will be a very little one, not big enough to spoil his dinner (he likes his dinner); while you, my poor soul, where will you be ?"

She has been lying with her head in my lap; at these last words she snatches it hurriedly up.

" What do you mean ?" she cries, in a fury. " How dare you pity me ? I am not a 'poor soul.' I am a very fortunate person—-very much to be envied. Hun-dreds of people would change places with me; so would you, if you could."

" Hm ! I don't know."

A pause.

" Lenore," say I, earnestly, putting my hand under her chin, and lifting her un-

willing face towards mine, " listen to me,
for I am talking sense. I never had a
husband, which is more my misfortune
than my fault, but all the same I know
what I am about. If you marry Charlie
now you will like him *at last;* I am sure
of that. I do not believe in the most per-
versely faithful woman *always* hating,
always having a distaste for a handsome,
manly, loving husband. Yes, you will end
by liking him even better than he does
you. It is always the way. But you will
have to go through purgatory first ; and,
what is more unfair, you will have to drag
him through too, poor boy !"

" Bah !" she says, with a scornful laugh ;
" it is nothing when you are used to it. If
I have not been there, I am sure I do not
know where I have been, ever since that
accursed ball. Shall I ever again hear
those detestable fiddles squeaking, and
those vile wind instruments blowing and

blaring, without going mad ?   I doubt it—
I doubt it !"—putting her hands wildly to
her ears, as if to shut out sounds of utter
pain and horror.

"You rather dislike him than otherwise now," pursue I, pushing my advantage ; "you are always better pleased to
see him leave a room than enter it ; well,
before your wedding tour is over, you
will *abhor* him.   It requires an immense
stock of love at starting to support the dead
sweet monotony of a honeymoon."

She shudders.

"My dear child," I cry, with affectionate
emphasis, "think better of it ; if you *must*
marry him—poor dear Charlie, I *am* sorry
for him—at least put it off for six months ;
let us have a little time to breathe.   If you
will reflect a moment I think you will see,
that to be handed on from one man to
another within a week is hardly ladylike,
hardly *modest !*"

At the last word the deep red on her cheeks grows yet deeper ; but by the hard defiant smile that curves her lips I know that I might as well have spoken to the winter wind that is howling and gnashing its angry teeth outside.

" Jemima," she says calmly, " as I once before observed to you, you will never make your fortune in the pulpit ; your sentiments are first-rate, but they make one drowsy. See, I am yawning, myself. As to *modest*, that is neither here nor there ; you dragged in the word by the head and shoulders to prop your argument. As to *ladylike*, it is a matter of the most perfect indifference to me whether I am or not."

To this I say nothing. I only walk away to the window.

" Do not dissuade me," she cries, falling from defiance to a tone of almost nervous entreaty, as she stands before me, twisting her hands. " Let me marry him in peace. Your little cut-and-dried saws are very neatly cut, very accurately dried, but they do not *fit;* you mean well, but one knows one's self best."

" Hm !"

" Do you think," she continues, with irritable impatience, " that I can go on *now* in the old groove—the old groove that I kept so contentedly to before—before the earth opened and swallowed all I had ?"

No answer.

" Can I go on," she pursues, with deepening agitation, " watching you drop the stitches in your knitting — listening to Sylvia's weak cackle—hearing those awful children plunging and bellowing about ? Do you know, Jemima, for the last few days, every time they have come blundering and shrieking into the room, I have felt inclined to scream out loud ? I have not done it, because you would have put me into a madhouse if I had ; but all the same, I have felt the inclination."

I shake my head despondently.

" If he marries me," she says, her eyes wandering restlessly about, and speaking quickly and excitedly, " he will take me away to beautiful places, away from all the dreadful old things and people.   It will be delightful—delightful !   I shall begin all over again—my life over again !   He will take me where there are no children—no Sylvias — no Jemimas — no self.   Yes " (laughing uneasily), " I mean to leave *myself* behind.   I mean to be a new, fresh person—a happy, prosperous person.   I *wish* to be happy—I am *determined* to be happy.   Jemima " (entreatingly) " for God's sake, do not hinder me !"

CHAPTER XVI.

WHAT THE AUTHOR SAYS.

NO one can keep their mouth open for ever — not even Jemima Herrick—they *must* shut it at last. Mostly they shut it very soon. No passion is so shortlived as astonishment. "A nine days' wonder" is a hyperbolical expression. Who ever wondered at the awfullest murder, the most startling *esclandre*, the most unlooked-for turn of Fortune's quick wheel, during nine whole days? If walking on your head were to come into fashion, within three days it would excite no surprise to see people

pounding along the pavement on their hats
and bonnets, with their boots in the
air. The neighbourhood has been informed of Lenore's transfer from one
lover to the other, and its " Ohs " and
" Ahs," and headshakings thereon are over
and done with. After all, they have been
fewer than might have been expected; people had so long made up their minds that
Scrope was the right man, that few of them
had arrived at the knowledge that he was
the wrong one, before they were officially
informed that he was the right one again.
He has always been seen about with her ;
he is evidently her fittest mate in youth
and comeliness ; in this case all the sympathy goes with the successful lover. Does
not he ride as straight as a die ? Is not he
as handsome as paint ? Do not we know
all his antecedents ? Does not his property
lie, does not his ugly old red abbey stand,
in this our county ? Paul, unknown, plain,

and saturnine, commands neither good wishes nor regrets. It has been announced that the engagement was dissolved by mutual consent—a course always adopted by the friends of the lady when the gentleman cries off. Lenore, however, is no party to this deception. Everybody's presents have been returned to them, and again sent back. On the principle of " To him that hath shall be given," the rich Mrs. Scrope's wedding gifts are threefold greater and more numerous than those of the poor Mrs. Le Mesurier. On hearing of the change in her fortunes—if not for the better, at least for the more consequential— the Websters supplement their portly teapot with a cream-jug and sugar-basin to match. And Lenore, when she sees the teapot come back—the teapot out of which she was to have poured Paul's tea, in the little narrow house they had planned—she laughs violently.

" Do not let them send me any new con-
gratulations—any of them," she says, dryly;
" tell them the old ones will do ; they need
only alter the *initials*, as I am doing with
my pocket-handkerchiefs."

Scrope has no father, and Lenore no
money, which two facts greatly facilitate
the law arrangements. Whether *indecently*
soon or not, the wedding day is drawing
on. Lenore has thrown herself into the
business of *trousseau* buying with an ardour
more than feminine—with the artistic frenzy
of a Frenchwoman, of a *petite maîtresse
enragée*.

" Finery always *was* my snare," she says,
laughing. " I loved even my cotton gowns
and gingham umbrellas tenderly, but *now*
—if being married, entails such a saturnalia
of fine clothes, I should like to have a
wedding every year."

Lenore is very lively ; she runs about
the house all day singing ; she walks, she

rides, she plays billiards; she studies 'Murray' and 'Bradshaw' with avidity, making out routes to the ends of the earth; but she *never* sits still. Her cheeks are rosy red, and her eyes sparkle and glitter like beautifullest great sapphires.

"You are quite the most *eager* bride I ever saw," Sylvia says one day, with a doubtful compliment. "Poor Charlie toils after you in vain. *I* always imagined that impatience was the monopoly of the gentleman; I am sure" (sighing and looking down) "it was so in my case. I thought the days *raced* by—positively *raced;* if you remember, Jemima, I said so to you at the time?"

"Did you? I dare say."

"Now Lenore, on the contrary, seems anxious to *hurry* them. Fancy!" casting up her eyes and hands to heaven.

"I *am* anxious," says the girl, smiling rather wistfully. "I mean to be so happy

—I want to begin. I am sorry it is not *en règle ;* but I cannot help that. How many more days are there ? One, two, three, four, five—bah !" (taking up two parcels that lie on the hall-table) "a couple more ivory prayer books ! Jemima, if there come any more prayer books you must send them back, and say that there is a glut of books of devotion."

The wedding feast is to be gay and large ; the house to be crowded and crammed from attic to cellar, chiefly with Scrope's people : mother, unmarried sister, married sister and husband, uncles, un-married men-cousins.

" A perfect horde of barbarians !" says Sylvia, complacently swimming into the drawing-room, on the afternoon of the day on which they are expected, her little figure very upright, head slightly thrown back, and bust protruded, as is her way when the war paint is on. " I have quite a good mind to run away and hide myself in a corner, and leave Tommy, as my deputy, to receive them. Will you, Tommy? How amusing it would be, and how astonished they would look !"

" One could hardly wonder at them," answers Jemima, dryly. Jemima's head and bust are much as usual.

" As long as I have Charlie beside me, I don't mind," continues Mrs. Prodgers, looking at herself over her left shoulder in the glass, in one of Silvy's strained and distorted attitudes; " he is my sheet anchor. Poor dear old Charlie !" (laughing a little) "to think of his going to be one's *brother !* It is *too* ridiculous !"

It is the evening before the wedding; the lit rooms are gaily alive with many guests; not only those staying in the house, but also dinner guests. Many more are expected; some of them already uncloaking outside, for Sylvia has decreed a dance.

"We must have a *band*," she has said, meditatively, when making the arrangements. "There is no use doing a thing unless you do it well. Yes, a band; they can go so nicely in the recess under the stairs."

"It *is* dreary work pounding over a carpet, to the tune of a piano, supported only by lemonade and negus," Jemima says.

"When people come on a *first* visit," says Sylvia sapiently, "they always come to criticise. Did you notice how they all looked me over from top to toe, when they came in to-day—*pricing* me, as it were? Well, I wish to be *beyond* criticism."

"Don't have a band," cries Lenore, hastily; "if you do, I shall go to bed—that is all. I warn you! Those dreadful fiddles squeaking and shrieking, go right through my head. Have a piano, and I will promise to play for you from now till the Judgment Day."

So a piano it is.   The dancing has not
yet begun, but we all stand about in an un-
settled way, that shows that *something* is
imminent.   Detachments of people are being taken to be shown the wedding presents.   The hot red roses have to-night
left Lenore's cheeks; she is very white—
deadly white, one would say; only that it
is a dishonour to the warm, milk whiteness
of *living* loveliness, to liken it to the hue
that is our foe's ensign.   She is pale, but
her eyes outblaze the star that quivers and
lightens in Mrs. Scrope's grey head.

" I am so glad you are not a *Mourning
Bride*," says Scrope's eldest sister, Mrs.
Lascelles, a frisky young matron, pretty as
hair like floss silk, Paris clothes falling off
her soft fat shoulders, and English jewels,
can make her, looking with a sort of in-
quisitive admiration at the restless pale
beauty of her future sister-in-law's face.
" Not that *I* can say anything " (laughing

lightly); " I cried for three whole days before *my* wedding. Mamma said that my
eyes looked as if they had been sewn in
with red worsted ; did not you mamma ?"

Mrs. Scrope smiles the placid smile of
prosperous stall-fed maturity.

" I did more than that," continues the
other, still laughing, " I cried for a fortnight afterwards ! We went to *Brittany* "
(making a disgusted face), "and Regy was
ill all the way from Southampton to St.
Malo. I tried to look as if he did not belong to me. I am sure even the waiters at
the hotels were sorry for me—I looked so
dejected ! "

At the mention of Brittany Lenore
winces, and then begins to talk quickly
and laughingly :

" *Must* one cry ? I hope not. If it is
indispensable I will *try ;* but I am afraid I
shall not succeed. I am not a good hand
at crying. I *never* cry."

They are to dance in the hall; the oak floor has been polished and doctored to the last pitch of slipperiness; the stags' heads have mistletoe wreaths. Plenty of light, plenty of warmth, plenty of space, plenty of men : what more can any rabid-est dance-lover desire? To the general surprise, Lenore sits down to the piano; everybody remonstrates.

" Usurping *my* place," says Jemima, cheerfully, putting her hands on her sister's shoulders. " Off with you."

" On the contrary," returns Lenore, with a perverse smile, " I mean to adorn this stool till two o'clock to-morrow morning. Go away—dance—caper about, if it amuses you; as for me, I hate it. *Va t'en !*".

" Come on !" cries Scrope, half in and half out of his grey gloves, and looking radiantly happy and handsome. " What do you mean by settling yourself there?

Jemima is going to play ; she always does ;
she likes it.   Don't you, Jemima ?"

Jemima smiles grimly.   All very well to
be conscious that your life mission is to
pipe for other people to dance, but a little
hard to be expected to express *enjoyment*
of the *rôle !*

" I am not going to ' *Come on !* ' " answers
Lenore, pettishly.   " I mean to stay here.
Go away !"

" *Go away !*" cries the young fellow,
leaning his arms on the piano, and looking
desperately sentimental ; " a very likely
story !"

" For Heaven's sake, put your head
straight !" she says, crossly.   " When you
cock it on one side like that, you look like
a bullfinch about to pipe.   I hate dancing !
--there !"

" Since when ?" he asks incredulously.
" Not long ago you told me that you loved
it better than anything else in life."

" Not so *very* long ago, when I was cutting my teeth, I loved sucking an india-rubber ring better than anything else in life. Do you insist on my sucking it still ?" she says dryly, turning over a heap of music. " Don't be a nuisance. Go away !"

He goes. In five minutes, all, not incapacitated by age and fat, and some even that lie under these disabilities, are scampering round. As there are plenty of men, several of the chaperones condescend to tread a measure. Lenore plays on dreamily ; it is an air that the band played at Dinan one night last summer ; as the brisk, gay melody fills her ears, the room, the people, the wax lights vanish ; she is in the Place Duguesclin again. How dark it is ! The lights from the hotel shew small and red ; the sabots clump past. How close to our faces the green lime flowers swing !

✳   ✳   ✳   ✳   ✳   ✳   ✳

She is roused by an eager voice at her ear.

" One turn—only one ! I have danced with everything that has any pretensions to age, weight, or ugliness. Pay me for it !— only *one* turn !"

Scrope stands by her, panting a little. His broad chest heaves, and his wide blue eyes glitter with a passionate excitement. She shrugs her shoulders, but, as though it were too much trouble to argue the point, complies. Jemima takes her place and they set off. After flying silently round for a few minutes they stop. Scrope, even in stopping, unwilling to release her from his arms, gazes into her face with a passionate rapture, to see whether the delight he feels is at all shared.

" I *hate* it !" she says irritably. " It tears my dress ; it loosens my hair ; it takes away my breath. Let us go to some cool place."

They saunter away to the conservatory.
The Chinese lanterns swing aloft, their
flames spiring up in dangerous proximity
to the pink and green walls of their frail
prisons. The daphnes and narcissi and
lilies of the valley are uniting their various
odours in one divinest harmony of scent,
like a concert of noblest voices. Lenore
throws herself wearily into a garden chair
and begins to fan herself.

" Let me fan you," says her lover tenderly, taking the fan out of her hand and
leaning over her, " it will save you trouble.
My darling, you look pale to-night."

"*My darling, you look red to-night,*"
retorts she, with a mockery more bitter
than playful, glancing up at the flushed
beauty of his face. " For Heaven's sake,
don't let us register the variations in each
other's complexions."

An arrow shoots through the young
man's bounding heart. Is she going to

change her mind ? Now that the prize is almost within his hand, must he lose it at this last moment ?

"Have I done anything to vex you?" he asks anxiously, kneeling down on the stone pavement at her feet. "You know how idiotically fond I am of you; for Heaven's sake, do not take advantage of it to play tricks with me! What is the matter with you to-night ? You are out of spirits."

"What do you mean ?" she cries angrily. "I never was in better spirits in my life; everybody remarks it—everybody says how lively I am. I talk all day, and I laugh more than I ever did in my life before. Would you have one always grinning like a Cheshire cat ?"

"You talk and laugh, it is true," he answers, with a grave air of anxiety, "but you are much thinner than you were. Look at this arm" (touching the round white

limb, as it lies listlessly across her lap) ;
"it is not half the size it was three weeks
ago."

"So much the better," she answers with
a laugh ; "my arms were much too big
before. Sylvia was always abusing them ;
it is much more refined to have smaller
arms."

"You will be all right when we get to
Italy," he says fondly ; "you will like that,
will not you ? Oh! sweet!" (leaning over
her, with a passion of irrepressible exulta-
tion) ; "can I believe that I am waking,
when I think that long before this time to-
morrow you will be my *wife ?*—that at last
—at last—we shall belong to one another,
for *always ?*"

She shivers a little. "To-day is to-day,
and to-morrow is to-morrow," she says,
sententiously ; "to-day, let us talk of to-
day ; we may both be dead by to-morrow."

" *Both !*" (smiling a little) ; " that is hardly likely."

" One of us, then ; only the other day I read in the *Times* of a bride who was found dead in her bed on her wedding morning. Oh, my God !" (flinging out her arms, and then throwing her head down on her knees,) " if I had but the very slightest chance of going to heaven, how I wish I could be found dead in my bed !"

" What are you talking about ?" cries Scrope, shocked and astonished at this unlooked-for outburst. " Lenore ! look me in the face and say you did not mean it. I know you have a random way of talking, sometimes—Jemima says so; but, do you know, when you say such things you break my heart ?"

" Do I ?" she says, lifting her wild white face, unsoftened by any tears. " I am glad. Why should not I break it ? I have broken my own—you know that well enough—why should not *you* suffer too? As for me, I suffer—I suffer always—all day and all night. I am glad to hear of any one else being miserable too. What have I done, that I should have a mono-poly of it?" He stares at her, in a stony silence. "There," she says, after a pause, with a sickly smile, pushing her hair off her forehead, "I am all right now! I was only—only—*joking!* Pay no attention to anything I said; I was only ranting. I think I have been overdoing myself a little the last few days. Suppose you go? I shall get well quicker if I am by myself."

So he goes, slowly and heavily. She has taken all the lightness out of his feet and out of his heart; it feels like a pound of lead. He makes his way up to the piano. "Jemima," he says, in a low voice, "my sister will play for you; I want you to go to Lenore; she is not very well, I think—rather hysterical ; she is in the conservatory, she would not let me stay with her."

So Jemima goes.

CHAPTER XVII.

WHAT JEMIMA SAYS.

"WHAT next?" think I, hurrying off, as bidden. "What new freak? Well, if I had been born with a silver spoon in my mouth I would not have spent my life in bewailing and lamenting that it was not a pewter one." In the conservatory no Lenore! Only two time-worn flirts of either sex, shooting their blunt little old arrows at each other's tough hearts, under a red camellia. I do not know why I do it, but I pass along, through the flowers, to a door at the other

end that gives upon the outer air, and
opening it, look forth.   It is snowing rather
fast : great, shapeless flakes floating down
with disorderly slowness ; but it is not very
dark.   My knowledge of my sister has not
been at fault, for, through the snow, I see
her, at a little distance from me, walking
quickly up and down a terrace walk, with
her head bent and her hands clasped before
her.   " How good for a person with a
weak chest !" I cry indignantly, skipping
gingerly out on the toes of my white satin
boots, and flinging the tail of my gown
adroitly over my head.   " Anyone more
unfit for death or more resolute to die than
you, I have seldom had the pleasure of
meeting."

I put my arm within hers and drag her
along, back into the lighted warmth of the
conservatory.   A great tier of orange trees
and chrysanthemums hides us from the
veteran lovers.   I look at her : the snow-

flakes rest thickly on her hair, on her flimsy dress; run in melted drops off her chilled white shoulders.

" It does not wet one much," she says, with a rather deprecating smile. " See, one can blow them away. How white they are ! They will make the snowdrops that the school-children are to strew before me to-morrow look quite dirty, will not they ?"

" Lunatic !" cry I, highly exasperated, shaking her ; "fool ! If I may be per-mitted to ask, what is the reason of this ?"

" I was hot," she says, a little wildly, " stifled ! Those flowers stifle me. Odious jonquils ! Did ever any flowers smell so heavily ? They are like the ones in that dreadful bouquet Charlie brought me for the ball."

I am shaking and flicking, with my best lace pocket-handkerchief, the snow from off her dress, so make no answer.

" You know, from a child, I was fond of running out, bare-headed, into a shower ; I liked to feel the great cool drops patter patter on my hair. I wish to God I could feel them now. Put your hand on my head" (lifting my cold, red hand, and placing it on the top of her own sleek head).

" My good child," say I, startled, "you are in a fever !"

" Jemima," she says, taking down my hand again, and holding it hard pressed between her two hot white ones, while her glittering eyes burn on my face, "I am quite happy, as you know, perfectly. No one has more cause to be so. I am quite young ; I am better looking than most people ; to-morrow I shall be rich, very rich ; which, after all, includes all the others ; but, do you know, sometimes, within the last few days, I have thought— it is a ridiculous idea, of course, but some-

times I have thought I was *going mad!*
How do people *begin* to go mad ? Tell
me ?"

Her voice has sunk to an awed whisper.
" Fiddlestick !" cry I contemptuously ; " do
not be alarmed, only clever people go mad ;
no fear for you."

" If anyone comes suddenly into a room,
if any one bangs a door, or speaks in a key
at all louder than usual, I feel as if I *must*
shriek out loud. I told you so the other
day, if you remember, talking of the
children ; sometimes I am afraid of lifting
my eyes to your or anyone else's face, for
fear you should think they *looked* mad."

" Nonsense," interrupt I again, now
thoroughly angry ; " it is all nerves !
Nerves are troublesome things if you are
not moderately careful of them, and you
never give yours a chance ; you never sit
still, you never rest, and it is my belief that
you never sleep."

" Not if I can help it," she says, feverishly; " not if I can help it. Sometimes,
when I feel myself falling asleep, I get out
of bed, and walk about in the cold to wake
myself thoroughly. I *hate* sleep; it is my
enemy! As sure as ever I fall asleep I am
back in Brittany with him; we are as—as
we used to be."

" If I were you," say I, with that sober
eye to the main chance with which one re-
gards life after five-and-twenty, " I should
be glad to wake from such a dream to find
how much more prosperous the reality is."

" So I am, so I am!" she answers
hastily, contradicting herself. " Of course!
it *is* prosperous, is it not? Everybody
says so; you—you are not *joking*, are you,
Jemima, when you say I am so prosperous?" (her eyes resting distrustfully on my
face). " I am *really*, am I not? But
sometimes I think, when I look at you,
that you are *pitying* me. Heaven knows

why! for nobody needs it less; if you are, do not—that is all! I hate being pitied; pity yourself instead."

"Dreams or no dreams," say I, trying to lead her from a theme which is making her painfully excited, "you *must* sleep to-night, if we give you laudanum enough to make seven new sleepers. If you do not, mark my words, to-morrow you will look as yellow as the little orange in your wreath." No answer, only a vacant pluck-ing at her dress. "Dead-white in the morning," say I, with a judicious adhesion to the subject of millinery, "is almost always fatally trying to the best com-plexions, particularly when in juxtaposition with snow." No answer. "Only this morning you told me that you were determined to look your very hand-somest."

"So I am," she says, rousing herself, and speaking with quick interest; "so I

am! You say right—I *must* look my best
- I shall; one always does when one
wishes; my veil will be down, too, they
will not see me very clearly, you know;
but, however I look, you must be sure to
have it put in the papers that I looked
beautiful and — and — radiantly happy.
They say those sort of things now and
then, do not they?"

" As to the being happy—never that I
saw," reply I, snappishly. " A bride's
happiness is taken for granted."

" I do not know whether I ever men-
tioned it to you before," she says, with a
hesitating strained smile, " but I should
like the announcement put into a good
many papers besides the *Times* — the
Morning Post—Standard; but it must be
in the *Times*, too, of course. People
always read the births, deaths, and marriages in the *Times*, don't they?"

She asks this last question with a keen

anxiety that would have puzzled any looker-on to account for.

" *Women* do," reply I brusquely. " I do not think that *men* ever look at them."

"What nonsense you talk!" she cries rudely. "Of course they do. They always glance over them, at the least, to see whether there is any name they know. I have seen them, a hundred times. I have seen Charlie——"

" What about Charlie ?" cries the young man, appearing round the screen of flowers simultaneously with his name ; " he has not done anything fresh, has he ?" (trying to laugh, but yet speaking with a most anxious smile). " Jemima, how is she ?— how are you now, my darling ?" taking her in his arms with as little heed to my presence as if I also were a prim dumb camellia.

" *How am I* ?" retorts she, pushing him

away with a gesture of distaste, and then, as if bethinking herself, accepting his embrace. "Why, how *should* I be ? Much as I have been any time these nineteen years, with the exception of the solitary week when I had the croup. Reassure yourself—I have not the croup now, and I never have any other diseases."

He looks at her silently, with a pale passionate wistfulness.

" You mean to be kind," she says, in a constrained voice, with a sort of remorse, "and you really are a very good fellow. I do think so always, though I show it rather oddly now and then perhaps ; but you must know that I have an inveterate aversion to being asked how I am. It is not confined to me. Many people have the same feeling. I really " (with a forced smile) " must draw up a list of prohibitions for you. ' You must not do this,' and ' You must not do that,' before we set off

on our travels, or we shall inevitably come
to blows before a week is over."

"*Do!*" cries the young man eagerly, as
one catching at a straw. "I do seem to
be always blundering, don't I? and saying
the wrong thing? One would think I did
it on purpose; but, as I live, I do not. I
shall get better, however," he continues,
hastily, as if afraid of her taking advantage of his confession; "every day I shall
get better. Being with you always, I shall
grow to understand your character better.
Dense as I am, I cannot help doing that,
can I, Jemima?"

"I really do not know," reply I, turning
away with a dry smile; "there are some
very sharp corners and unexpected turns
in it, I can assure you."

"Jemima is right," says Lenore, gravely,
gently unwinding his arms from about her.
"You have got a very indifferent bargain,
pleased as you are with it. To let you

into a secret, you have overreached yourself. You will get a bad character of me
from all the people I have spent my life
with ; I have the distinction of having
everybody's ill word."

"I dare say" (defiantly, while his eyes
recklessly, boundlessly fond, grow to her
calm, chill face).

"It is not too late yet," she says, in a
low voice that has yet nothing of the
whisper in it ; "it is one o'clock ; I hear it
striking. You have yet ten hours' grace."

"Ten hours!" cries the young fellow,
wildly, throwing his arms again about her,
and straining her, whether she will or no,
to his riotous heart. "Lenore! Lenore!
the nearer the time grows the farther you
seem to get away from me. Are you
going to slip away from me altogether at
the last moment, as you did out of my
arms just now ? But no !—why do I put
such ideas into your head ? It is too late.

You could not throw me over now, if you wished. Reckless as you are of all conventionality, even you dare not do that."

" What are you talking about ?" she asks, petulantly, with a nervous laugh. " Why should I wish to throw you over ? If I did, what could I do with all my fine clothes, and my otter-skin jacket ? Do you think I could have strength of mind to send the Websters' teapot travelling back a *second* time ?"

He continues looking at her, and holding her, but says nothing.

" I *like* you," she says, looking round at me with a sort of nervous defiance. " I do not care who says I do not. I am proud of you—I—I—I *love* you. Do not I, Jemima ? Have not I often told you that I do ?"

" You have told me a great many things in your time," I say, oracularly, " some that were true and some that were not. I

will tell you one thing in return, and that
is, that if you do not go to bed now, this
minute, to-morrow you will be yellower
than any orange."

CAPPTER XVII.

WHAT JEMIMA SAYS.

T is a circumstance never to be enough deplored by the female world that marriages and drawing rooms are broad daylight ceremonies. Mature necks and faces, that the great bold sun makes look as yellow as old law deeds or as the love letters of twenty years ago, would gleam creamily, waxily white, if illumined only by benevolent candles, that seem to see and make seen only beauties and slur over defects. Even the lilies and roses of youth—unlike the smooth perfec-

tion of their garden types—are conscious of
little pits and specks and flaws when day
holds his great searching lamp right into
their faces.   Day repudiates tulle and tarle-
tane; they are none of his; and as he cannot rid himself of them he retaliates by
behaving as glaringly and unhandsomely
as he can to them.   Nature is holding a
wedding outside too, apparently; at least,
it is all white, *white!*   Heaven has sent
down a storm of diamonds in the night, as
a marriage present to Lenore; wherever
you look there is the glitter of myriad bril-
liants.   Last night, at each iron gate, there
was a high wide arch of evergreens, but
during the dark hours the fairies carried
the dingy things away, and replaced them
by others of glistening white jewels.   They
are so bright, so bright, one cannot look at
them; one turns away with winking eyes.
I fancy that with some such lustre shine
the archways through which the Faithful

People go and come in the deathless white City of God.

There is a nuptial stir and bustle in the house ; everybody but the bride has been down to an early breakfast, and has gone up again to put their best clothes on. The maid servants are hurrying about the house in uniform grey gowns and white caps, all except the ladies' maids, who have the right of exercising individual will in the choice of their magnificence. The footmen have new liveries. The wedding-breakfast is laid out in the dining-room ; I have been reconnoitring it. One has to look out of window to assure oneself that the season is winter. On the long glittering table summer and autumn hold their scented sway. Regiments of tall flowers—both white and vivid-coloured ; shady fern forests, bunches of grapes, big as those fabulous ones swinging in gilt over an ale-house door, or as that mighty cluster represented in the illus-

trations to 'Line upon Line,' as borne between two stout Hebrews, slung upon a
pole; odorous rough-skinned pines. I in-
dulge in a pleased sigh, and glance at the
carte. I draw a slight mental sketch of
what my own share in the banquet will be.
Truly, one waxes gluttonous in one's old age.

Since then I have been pervading such
of the ladies' rooms as intimacy gives me
the *entrée* to. I have seen twelve passably
fair maids, in twelve gauzy bonnets, each
with a murdered robbin sitting on the top,
as a delicate tribute to the season. Pretty
and clean and white the dozen look; but,
alas! they will present but a drabby-grey
appearance by-and-by out of doors, when
contrasted with the wonderful blinding
snow-sheet. I am not a bridesmaid: I
have not been invited, nor, if I had, would
I have consented to intrude the washed-
out pallor of my face among this plump
pink rose garden.

Now I have returned to the bride chamber, where Sylvia, fully dressed, and apparently labouring under some hallucination as to being herself the bride, has usurped the cheval glass; at least, on my entry, I find a pretty little figure in violet velvet and swansdown, with bust protruded and semi-dislocated neck, gyrating slowly before it.

" How extraordinary one does feel in *colours !*" she is ejaculating, with a sort of uneasy complacency; "but for Lenore's sake, nothing should have induced me. I feel quite like a fish out of water; I really can hardly believe it is my own face—it seems like some one else's. What a fright one does look, Jemima!"

No contradiction from me.

" Does not one ?"

" No, I don't think so," reply I consolingly; "nothing out of the way. I don't see much difference."

" Violet always *used* to be considered my. colour," returns Sylvia, apparently finding my form of comfort not very palatable; "always *par excellence.* How well I remember, the very last ball I ever went to with poor Tom—I was in violet *lisse,* with cowslips—overhearing some man ask, 'Who that lovely little woman in mauve was?' What a rage I was in !"

" And who *was* she ?" ask I, with interest.

" *Who was she ?*" (reddening). " What stupid questions you do ask, Jemima ! *Who was she ?* Why *I,* of course."

" Mauve suits everybody, even *me,*" say I, peeping over Sylvia's shoulder at my own unusual lilac splendour, " it was well-named the 'refuge of the destitute.' "

Having discharged this Parthian shaft I turn away. The room is blocked with great imperials, packed and half-packed. A whole haberdasher's shop of finery is surging out of them, and a big white L. S. is on each of their shiny black lids.   L. S. herself sits before the dressing-table, but —difficult as it is to help it—she is not looking at herself in the glass.   Her eyes are on the ground and her brows gathered. She is fully dressed, with the exception of the wreath and veil ;—all dead white— dead white, like the doll on the top of a twelfth-night cake ; only that the doll in- · variably compensates for the colourlessness of her attire by cheeks that outshine the peony, and *Lenore's* cheeks are dead white too.   To my mortification, I perceive, that in spite of Worth's gown, and old Mrs. Scrope's Flemish point, my sister is look- ing as little handsome as a thoroughly good-looking woman ever *can* look. Hardly a touch of pretty red, even on her lips, and a pinched blue look of cold and utter apathy about her face and whole attitude.

"If I am to arrange your wreath," say I, speaking sharply, "we had better begin; there is no use hurrying, and it takes some time to dispose it properly."

She does not move or change her position.

"Will you be good enough," continue I, ironically, "to look round and convince yourself that this is not a funeral?"

Still no answer.

"Lenore" (raising my voice), "are you dead? are you dumb? are you cataleptic? For heaven's sake, why do you not say something?"

"What *should* I say?" she answers, at length, raising her heavy eyes, and speaking with harsh irritability; "why *should* I speak? I have only *one* hour more of my own now" (glancing with a sort of tremulous shudder towards the clock); "surely I may spend it as I like."

"That is better," rejoin I, not heeding

the matter of her speech, but regarding her, with my head on one side, with an artist's eye. "When you speak you look ten per cent. better. I must tell you in confidence that as you sat just now, with your shoulders up to your ears and your nose resting on your knees, you had a near escape of being that anomaly in nature, a plain bride."

No reply.

"For mercy's sake, say something," I cry, crossly; "do not lapse again into that utter silence! Dear me!" (taking the wreath gingerly out of its box) "how beautifully they do make these things nowadays! But for the scent, I really think they out-do nature."

The wheels of the first carriage become audible; very faintly, by reason of the snow, but still audible, and Sylvia, after one final glance, shuffle, and whisk, swims out of the room. I become absorbed in an

artistic agony, as I throw the lace, in a
shower of costly flimsiness, over my sister's
impassive head, and delicately insinuate
the chilly nuptial flowers into their resting-
place on the top of it.

Carriage after carriage rolls up : doors
are opened ; steps let down.   My curiosity
gets the better of me.   I leave my nearly
finished task, and, running to the window, press my face against the frosted
pane.

" The Websters," say I, narratively.
" Ha ! ha ! ha ! Old Mrs. Webster in a
twin gown to Sylvia ; even to the swansdown on the body and tunic !   Poor dear
Sylvia ! she will never get over it ; it will
be the death of her."

As I stand there, laughing, maliciously,
I feel a hand on my shoulder.   "What !
are *you* come to look at them, too ?   Take
care, they will see you.   It shows a little
want of imagination in Mrs. James making

two dresses pin for pin alike, does not
it ?"

I turn towards her ; but, as soon as I
catch a glimpse of her face my mirth dies,
and I utter a horrified ejaculation. It is
lividly white, and she is gasping.

" Open it wide !" she says, almost inaudibly. " I—I—I am stifling !"

" Good heavens !" cry I, apprehensively
and dissuasively, with my usual practical
grasp of a subject. " You are not going
to faint ? Do not !—not till I get you a
chair. You are so heavy—I never could
hold you up."

As I speak I am struggling with the
hasp of the window, which is old, rusty,
and evidently constructed with a view to
never opening except after ten minutes of
angry wrestling.

" Quick ! quick !" she says, faintly, panting, " wider ! *wider !*"

But it is too late. As the frozen case-

ment grates slowly on its hinges, her head,
with all its smart paraphernalia of lace and
flowers, falls back lifeless, and the whole
weight of her body, in all the leaden inert-
ness of Death's counterfeit, rests in my
strained arms.   No one knows, until they
have tried it, how heavy dead and swooned
persons are.   I stagger under my sister's
weight, and with much difficulty, and many
bumps both to her and myself, get her
down on the floor, where the little icy airs
come and ruffle her useless laces and her
soft tossed locks.   Then I fly to the bell,
open the door, and call mightily down the
passage.   " Louise !" I cry, " Louise !" as
Sylvia's French maid comes floating airily
along—not in the least hurrying herself,
but rather throwing gallantries over her
shoulder, as it were, to a strange valet in
the middle distance.   " Louise ! Louise !
Make haste ! Mademoiselle Lenore is so
ill ! I do not know what has happened to

her !—all of a sudden, too !—she has fainted, I think ; I suppose it *is* a faint, is not it ?" (looking nervously in her face) " not anything *worse ?*"

Louise gives a little yell, and says " My God !" in her mother tongue, in which flippant language that adjuration does not sound half so solemn. Then we kneel down, one on each side of her, sprinkle water in her face, considerably to the injury of her tucker—pour brandy down her unconscious throat—hold strong smelling-salts to her nostrils—roughly chafe her dead hands—use all the unpleasant asperities, in fact, that are supposed necessary to induce people to come back to that life which, as a rule, they are so loth to quit. But it is all to no purpose : she shows no sign of returning consciousness.

" I do not half like it," I say, looking apprehensively across at my coadjutor, and speaking in an unintentional whisper. " I have not a notion what to do next! Run, Louise, and tell John to go as quickly as he can for Dr. Riley—and—and—I do not like being left here by myself with her— send Mrs. Prodgers."

" What do you want with me ?" cries Sylvia, pettishly, coming fussing in, a minute or two later; evidently in complete ignorance of the errand on which I have sent for her.

" I wish you would not send such mysterious messages. I am so nervous already that I do not know what to do with myself! I declare, just now, when Lord Sligo was talking to me, I had no more idea what he was saying —— Good God !" (catching sight of Lenore's stiff prostrate white figure), " what has happened ? What has she done to herself now ?"

" She has fainted," repeat I, briefly, " all of a sudden, before I could look round ; and we cannot bring her to."

"Good gracious, how dreadful!" cries Sylvia, kneeling daintily down on the floor too, not however, before she has plucked up her violet velvet skirts. "What does one do when people faint?—put cold keys down their backs—cut their stay-laces— hold looking-glasses before their mouths— oh no, of course, that is to see whether they are — heavens, Jemima," (her face blanching), "you do not think she is "——

Mrs. Prodgers has an inveterate aversion for pronouncing the little four-lettered word, that, in its plain shortness, expresses the destiny of the nations.

"Nonsense!" cry I, angrily, again seizing the salts, and futilely holding them to her nose.

"Feel whether her heart beats," says Sylvia, looking very white, breathing rather short, and speaking in an awed whisper. "I am afraid to do it myself—I dare not!—you are feeling the wrong side, are not you ?—they say it is nearly in the middle."

Complying with these anatomical instructions, I feel. Yes, it beats. Life's little hammer is still knocking feebly against its neighbour ribs.

" She will be all right, just now, of course ; it is only that we are not used to this sort of things. I never was the least frightened myself," say I, doughtily, but not altogether truly.

" I wish her eyes were *quite* shut," says Sylvia, peering into Lenore's swooned face with the horrified curiosity of a child ; " they look so dreadful showing a bit of the pupil."

" The wedding will have to be put off, of course," say I, rising, and walking towards the clock ; " half-past eleven now ; it is very certain that she will not be well enough to be married before twelve."

" But the *people !*" cries my sister, squatting in a dismayed purple heap on the floor, for the moment utterly oblivious of nervousness, swansdown, or even of the aptness of velvet to crease, unless sat upon straight. " They are all come; everybody is dressed ; most of them are already at the church ; the bishop has been there half an hour."

I shake my head. " It cannot be helped."

" And the breakfast !" cries Mrs. Prodgers, as a fresh and worse aspect of the calamity presents itself to her mind. " Of course, the cold things do not matter ; they will be as good to-morrow or the day after as to-day ; but the soups, the *entrées !*"

I stifle a sigh. " There is no good in talking of it," I say, with forced philosophy. " You had better go at once and send them all away ; there is no use in keeping them waiting in the cold. Charlie, too " (with an accent of compassion); " poor boy !

what a bitter disappointment it will be to
him !"

" As to that," says Sophia, with a slight
relapse into the preening and Pouter-pigeon
mood, " I do not suppose that a day's delay
will kill him : men are often not sorry for
a little reprieve in these cases. I am sure
no one can feel more thoroughly upset than
I do; if I were to follow my own inclina-
tions I should sit down and have a good
cry."

" Do not follow them then," I say
brusquely, " or, at least, send the guests
away *first*, and cry as much as you please
afterwards."

By the aid of Louise, and with many
appeals on her part to the French God,
skies, and Virgin, I heavily and with difficulty, lift Lenore on to the bed. Hours
have passed, the doctor has come, Sylvia
has resumed her black gown and giant
rosary, the last carriage has rolled away

with snowy wheels, before Lenore lifts the quivering white of her lids, and looks round upon us languidly, one after another. There are only three of us—the elderly doctor, to whom from our earliest infancy we have been in the habit of exhibiting our tongues and pulses, I, who am nobody, and thirdly, a poor young man in a smart blue coat, with a kind, miserable, beautiful face, who has spent the last three hours and a half in clasping and kissing a limp white hand, which, had its owner been possessed of consciousness, would hardly have lain with such passive meekness in his fond grasp. As her eyes open he springs up joyfully to his feet and bends over her. I do the same. With a faint gesture of dis-taste she turns away from him to me, and speaks in a weak whisper :

"I—I—I—am at home, am I not ?"

"*At home?* Yes, to be sure."

"I—I—I am not *married?*"

6—2

" No, not yet."

" I am so glad !"

Soon afterwards she relapses into un-
consciousness. All that day, and most of
the following night, she lies like a plucked
snowdrop in January's sleety lap, reviving
from one swoon only to fall into another.
Towards midnight she grows better, and
sinks into a natural and healthy sleep.

" I wish you would change your clothes,"
I say to Charlie, in a whisper, as we stand
staring at her with shaded light, "they
look such a mockery " (touching the fine
blue broadcloth). " Your poor bouquet,
too."

" Not a very good omen, is it ?" he says,
with a melancholy smile, lifting with his
finger the drooped and yellow head of his
gardenia. " Bah ! who cares for omens ?
Only old women."

" Only old women," repeat I, mechanically.

"She was not well *last night*," he continues eagerly, " was she ? I told you she
was not : it accounts for her talking so
oddly, does not it ? It shows " (peering
anxiously into my face) " that she did not
mean any of the things she said, does not
it ?"

I say, "Of course," in a constrained
voice, and try to turn away.

" Stay," he says, laying his broad hand
on my shoulder, "do not go ; I want to
talk to you. I say she was not quite herself when she woke up first, was she ?—
did not know what she was saying—*meant*
nothing ?"

I know that I am lying, but I answer :
" Oh dear, no ! of course not !"

" Was it my fancy ?" continues he, with
a painful red spreading even to his forehead ; " one gets odd notions, and these
damned candles " (striking one viciously
with his forefinger) " cast such deceptive

shadows—but it seemed to me, Jemima, that she turned away from me, as if—as if —she had rather not look at me. Did not she like my being here, do you think? She is so—so—*maidenly;* she thought I ought to have staid outside?"

"Nonsense," say I, shortly. "It is evident that you have never fainted; you do not understand how slow people's wits are in coming back. I do not suppose that she knew you from me, or me from the doctor."

He does not answer. I can hardly expect my logic to be very convincing, seeing that it has not convinced myself.

"Riley is not in the least surprised at this," I say, nodding slightly towards our patient. "When I told him about her not eating and not sleeping—it is my belief that she has not closed an eye for the last fortnight—he said that the only wonder was that it had not happened before."

"Jemima," says the young fellow, turning me unceremoniously round so as to face him, while his eyes in their searching truth go through mine like swords, "tell me—I wish to know—what is it that has taken away her sleep and her appetite? Is it *I*?"

It is not, as I am well aware, but I maintain a stupid silence.

"Do not answer me," he says, with a sudden change of mood, pushing me away from him. "I do not want an answer; it was an idiotic question; this fuss and bustle have been too much for her, have not they? and the hard weather has tried her. She will be all right again when once we get quietly off, will not she? Jemima—I say, Jemima—do you think there is a chance of our being able to have it to-morrow?"

I shake my head. "I doubt it."

"The· day after, then?" (very wistfully).

I have not the assurance to say " Yes,
and I have not the heart to say " No," so
I say, " We will see."

CHAPTER XIX.

WHAT THE AUTHOR SAYS.

ALL the next day Lenore lies in bed, weak and white—it does not take much to pull her down —and, for the most part, silent. She asks for no one; expresses neither regrets nor self-congratulations on the subject of her deferred wedding—lies with her face, gentle and innocent as any saintly martyr's—what falsehoods faces do tell!—on the pillow, crowned by a bright brown glory of hair— an aureole given her by nature, not martyrdom. She is not ill, neither well; very

still, and only turning restive under doses
of brandied beef-tea, repeated *ad nauseam.*
There are few of the minor diseases that
are worse than beef-tea and brandy.   The
following day passes in much the same
way; but on the third morning Jemima
enters cheerfully :

" Riley says you may get up."

The communication does not seem to
afford much satisfaction to the person to
whom it is addressed.   She turns her face
away with a pettish jerk and hides it in
the pillow.

" He says you may dress and come
down as soon as you like."

"*As soon as I like ?*" repeats Lenore,
ironically ; " that would be a long time off.
Why may not I stay here ?"—(stretching
out her arms lazily).   " I am happy.   I
like to lie here all day long; the noises of
the house seem so far off, and your footsteps outside sound so gently.   I like to

listen to the clocks one after another, and count them as they strike. I feel nothing —I think of nothing. I have not been so happy for years."

"He says that staying in bed is very weakening."

"Then I like being weakened."

"Nonsense! Please talk like a rational being."

Never was toilet more slowly made than Lenore's—partly from weakness—for her illness, though brief, has told upon her; partly from a deep and innate unwillingness to return to the well and work-a-day world. At length there is no evading the fact that she is fully dressed; not only fully dressed, but established in an arm-chair before Sylvia's boudoir fire : a banner screen between her face and the flame ; novels, workboxes, point lace, a pug—everything that is necessary to make a rational woman's happiness—within easy reach of

her hands.   There is one other addition,
without which, many rational women think
happiness incomplete—a lover ; and even
he is not far off.

As a man's heavy step sounds muffled
along the carpeted passage, as a man's
fingers close on the door-handle, Lenore
turns her head resolutely to the other side
—like a child averting its face from the
inevitable rhubarb and magnesia—and rests
her cheek on the back of her chair.

He enters softly, and afraid even of
breathing over-noisily, imagining she is
asleep, stoops his waved gold head over
her.   He is soon undeceived.

" I wish," she says, in a most wide-awake
voice, opening her beautiful petulant eyes
full upon him, "that you would not come
in, in that creakily tiptoe way; nothing in
the world fidgets me so much."

He starts upright again in a hurry.

" It was a stupid trick," he says humbly,

and then stops suddenly, afraid of rousing livelier wrath by further speech. As for her, she rolls her pretty pettish head from side to side, and affects not to see him. He grows tired at last, of standing with his back to the mantelshelf, silent, and says, with eager tenderness but in a rather frightened voice :

" You are better ?"

" Yes, I am better," she answers, quickly; "at least, so they say ; but I am still far from well—very far ; it will be long enough before I am strong again, and—and—and —up to anything."

" Riley says that there is nothing like— like *change of air*" (reddening guiltily).

"Riley is an old woman" (reddening too).

" Lenore !" throwing himself down on his knees, on the rug beside her, and in so doing, giving an unconscious buffet to the pug's black face, who forthwith departs

howling, unheeded, and with his tail un-
curled. "Lenore! why need we have half
the county to see us married? Why need
we put on smart clothes? Why cannot
you come quietly to church with me to-
morrow, in your common bonnet and
shawl" (Scrope is unaware that shawls are,
for the moment, extinct,) "with only the
clerk to say 'Amen'"

"Where is the hurry?" she asks, tapping
her foot impatiently on the fender. "You
talk as if we were two old people, each
with a leg in the grave. Supposing that
we put it off for a year, we should still
probably have fifty to gape opposite each
other in."

"Even if we were sure of the fifty," he
says gently, "I should still grudge the one;
can one be *too long* happy?"

"I never heard any one complain of
being so."

"Do you like sickly women?" she says,

abruptly, apparently half softened by his tone and looking amicably at him. " I think I am radically sickly—see how half a day has pulled me down—my elbows stick out like promontories " (pulling up her sleeve to show one)—" if you married me you would have to be always *cosseting* me —trundling me about in a Bath chair, and measuring out physic in a spoon for me."

He is about to burst into a storm of protestations, but she interrupts him.

" Do you know what Jemima said, that day, when I told her I was going to marry you ?"

" No."

" Well, she said it was *indecently* soon."

" I do not see what business it was of Jemima's," says the young man, looking rather surly.

" Neither do I ; but all the same it is true—*indecently* soon—that is the very word that expresses it." As she speaks, her face becomes spread with a hot blush, and his own is not slow to repeat it in the deeper colours of manhood.

"What does this mean ?" he asks, rising to his feet, while a look of utter fear makes the red in his cheeks give way. "What is this the preface to ?   Is it *indecently* sooner than it was yesterday, or the day before, or the day before that ?"

"Do not be angry," she says deprecatingly, stretching out her hand on which his own diamonds are flashing. "You know you are always reasonable — you always mind what I say, even when it is not reasonable ; that is why I like you."

There is something of the turkey-cock about every woman ; gobbling and swelling if a man is frightened and runs ; small and silent if he stands still and cries "Shoo !" It is his turn now ; there is no use in gobbling at him ; he affects not to see her hand, and only says briefly, " Go on."

" You know," she says, sitting upright in her chair and straining her neck backwards, so that her eyes may attain his face and watch it, " that I proposed to you—it is not a sort of thing that a man would be likely to forget. I try to think of it as little as possible, but it is true ; and you accepted me ;—I suppose " (laughing, awkwardly) " that you could not well have been so uncivil as to do otherwise."

" Go on."

" Well " (fidgeting uneasily), " I mean to marry you still—*fully*—but—but—it must be—not just yet—not now ; a year—six months hence, perhaps—instead."

Unwilling to witness the effect of her words, she has dropped her eyes at the last clause ; but as the moments pass, and no sound comes, save that of a cinder falling from the grate, she looks up again.

"Have you no tongue?" she says, irritably; "are you *never* going to speak?"

"*A year hence!*" he says, in a low voice, turning a face, white as the face of the uncoloured dead, towards her. "That means *never*. Thank you for leading me so gently up to it. Do you think I do not see what you are aiming at? Do you think I have not watched it coming during the last fortnight? I have prayed not to see" (striking his hands together). "I have entreated God to let me be blind always. Good God!" (flinging his arms down on the chimneypiece, and hiding his face on them) "how do men bear these things? Who can teach me?"

"Bear what?" she cries, rising hastily to her feet, and putting her hand on his coat sleeve. "What are you talking about? What is there to bear?"

"So you have been tricking me all this time, have you?" he says, raising his ruffled head, and looking deliberately at her, with a resentful calm in face and voice. " At least, it can hardly be called trickery : it was so lamely done, a child might have seen through the deception.".

Silence.

" Of course you know best " (in the same polite, cold tone) ; " but would it not have been simpler, and come to much the same thing in the end, to have left me alone in the first instance ?"

Left him alone ! The very question, in almost the same words, that Paul had once asked.

" I had gone clean away," he continues, in the same repressed and sedulously quiet voice. " Your polite speeches had effectually rid you of me. A man would not willingly listen *twice* to some of the compliments you paid me at that ball. I had no intention of coming back ; why did you send for me ?"

Still no answer, no attempted defence.

" I can at least" (with a bitter smile, that sits ill on his fair smooth face) " pay you the compliment of saying that you are not a *good* liar. You are not apt at the trade ; you bungle. Every day, and fifty times a day, your *mouth* has said to me, ' I like you—you are a good fellow—we shall be happy together;' and every day, and fifty times a day, your eyes and every movement of your body have said, ' I *loathe* you. I can hardly bring myself to speak civilly to you.' "

Still silence.

" Did it ever occur to you" (taking her by both slender wrists) "to make a rough calculation how many falsehoods you have told me during this last month ?"

"Stop !" she cries, wrenching away her hands from his grasp, which has more of the gaoler than the lover in it. " Stop ! you are very bitter to me—very. I can hardly believe that it is you ; but you speak truth. I *have* told you many, many lies, but at least I have told them to my-self too. I have said them over and over again, in the hope that they would come true at last."

He smiles a dry smile of utter incre-dulity.

" That was very probable."

" You do not believe me ?" she says, passionately. " Well, *I take God to witness* —you will hardly disbelieve me now—that ever since that day in the library, when I thrust myself so immodestly on you " (she is crimsoner than any closed daisy's petals at the words), " I have longed and striven with all my heart and soul and strength to —to—care for you—as—as—you wish to be cared for."

" Well ?"

" I have said over and over to myself all your good qualities, like a lesson. I have tried " (her face contracts with an agony of shame) "to wrench away all the love I ever had to give from—the—the person who once had it, and to give it to you instead."

" Well ?"

" Sometimes, when I was away from you, I thought I had succeeded ; but when you came near me, when you touched me, good and kind and handsome as you are——"

She stops abruptly.

" Go on," he says, in a hoarse whisper. " Do not let any consideration for my feelings stop you ; it would not be *you* if you did—*good and kind and handsome as I am*" (ironically repeating her words).

" It was too soon—too soon," she cries, clasping her hands in deep excitement, while the large scalding tears drop hotly over her cheeks. " Jemima was right, it was *indecently* soon.   In the grief and shame of being so treated, I wonder, Charlie" (smiling painfully), "that you are so anxious to marry a *jilted* woman. I thought I could forget all in a minute, but I cannot; nobody could. If I were to go away to-day, and throw you over for ever, could *you* forget *me* all in a minute?"

" I would try my best," he says, with a fierce white smile. " Perhaps it would be more correct to say, 'I *will* try my best.'"

" Do you think I do not *wish* to forget?" she says, taking his hand of her own accord, while her wet eyes gaze wistfully upward, into the deep angry blue of his. " Do you think I remember *on purpose?* Does one *enjoy* not sleeping and not eating, and being in miserable uneasy pain all day and all night?"

He keeps silence.

" I am no great prize at the best of times," she says, half sobbing. " My sisters

—all my people—will tell you that; but what sort of woman should I have been if I could have jumped straight out of one man's arms into another's, quite easily and comfortably, without feeling any shame? It was bad enough to be able to do it at all. Oh, Charlie! Charlie! knowing what you did about me, how could you think me worth taking? How could you take me?"

"*How could I take you?*" he says, with a harsh low laugh, as unlike the jocund sound of his usual boyish mirth as possible. "Do not you know that when a man is *starving* he is not particular as to having a *whole* loaf? He says 'thank you' even for *crumbs*. I tell you, Lenore, that morning in Ireland, when I got your note, I had as little hope of ever holding you in my arms as my wife, as I had of holding one of God's angels. When I found that there was a chance of my so holding you, judge whether I was likely to throw it away."

He has put one of his hands on each of her shoulders, and stands gazing stead-fastly at her with a bitter yearning in his eyes.

" I knew that your *soul* was out of my reach," he continues, sadly ; "that I should get only your body, and even *that* shrank away from me. Shall I ever forget those first two kisses that you gave me—that I *made* you give me ? They were colder than ice."

A little pause. The fire-flame quivers and talks to itself; the pug plucks up heart again, and, returning, lies down, with his nose resting on his bowed forelegs.

" I suppose it is all for the best," says Scrope, presently, with a forced smile ; "at least it is as well to say so, is not it ? I was so idiotically fond of you that, if you had been decently civil to me, I suppose I should have been happier than any man can be and live." No answer. "Do you know," he resumes, in a tone of deep and sombre excitement, "what has kept me up all this month, what has hindered me from cutting my own throat or yours—it was a toss-up which—what has made me smile and seem pleased at words that *bit* and looks that *stung*? Well, I will tell you—listen, and laugh if it amuses you; it is true, all the same. I *knew*" (lifting his hands from her shoulders, and framing her drooped face with them,) "I *knew* that, if once I could get you all to myself, I could *make* you love me; you would do your best to thwart and hinder me, but I could *make* you. Lenore, I know it still."

"Do you?" she says sadly. "I wish you could; but I doubt it."

"Tell me," cries the young fellow, emboldened by her gentleness to take her once more in his arms, as if she were his

own, " it will do me no good to hear—be
tantalising, rather — but still I think it
would ease my pain a little ; tell me, if
you had met me *first*—met me before you
came across *him*—do you think you could
have liked me a little *then?* Say ' yes,' if
you can, Lenore !" (with a suffering accent
of entreaty).

"How do I know?" she says sharply,
for once not shrinking from his contact—
not struggling in his embrace, but rather
coldly taking it for granted. " What is the
good of looking back? It seems to me
now, that if I had not met *him* I should
have gone on always, as I had gone on
before, laughing and amusing myself, and
being happy in my way, and not loving
anybody *much*. I never was one to fall in
love *easily*—never !" (drawing herself up
with a little movement of pride).

"You fell in love with *him* easily
enough," says Scrope, roughly.

"Yes," she answers, almost humbly, though her face flames, " you are right, so I did; it was a boast I had no right to make."

" What on earth made you do it ?"

" How can I tell ? Perversity, I think; I always was perverse from a child; they said I should pay for it, sooner or later. I think I have now, have not I ?" (smiling drearily). A moment's pause. " Other people cared for me of their own accord," she continues, sighing ; " as for him, almost every word I said *grated* upon him ; I had to fight and battle even for his toleration."

" And *that pleased* you ?"

" Does one ever care for the things that one can stretch out one's hand and take ?" she asks, bitterly. " I do not, neither do you—that is evident, or you would not be here." After a little pause : " He thought very meanly of me from the first—very.

He almost told me so in so many words, and I—I—well—I only meant to make him alter his mind ; that was how it began. Bah !" (breaking off suddenly, with a tempest of angry pain in her voice,) " what does it matter how it began ? Is not it enough that it *did* begin, that it went on, and that now it is *ended* ?"

At the last word her raised voice sinks down, and dies in a sob. His hold upon her grows lax, he gives a long sigh of astonished indignant grief.

" If that was the way to your heart," he says with a sort of scorn, " no wonder I missed it." Silence. " Merciful heavens !" cries the young man, smiting his hands together in a sort of wondering frenzy, " did one ever hear the like ? Must one hold you cheap, and have the ill manners to tell you so ; must one cut you to the heart with frosty looks and words that *stab* like your own ; must one love you tardily and leave you readily, before you will give one your affection ? If so, Lenore, I tell you candidly that—stark staring mad about you as I have been for the last six months—I tell you candidly that I had rather be without it."

" You are right," she says, coldly ; " it is not worth having. After all, you agree with him ; *he* thought it was not worth having, and so threw it away."

The moments flash past ; the little moments, that tarry not to listen to brisk wedding chimes, or the slow passing-bell. The two young people still stand opposite one another, each buried in thoughts, whereof it would be hard to say whose share was the bitterer. Scrope is the first to break the silence that has fallen on them.

" Tell me, Lenore," he says, breaking out into impetuous speech, "you have said so many disagreeable things to me in your

time that *one* more will not matter ; yes,
tell me—I will promise not to burst out
into violence, I will even try to look
pleased" (smiling [sardonically)—" is there
—is there—any talk of *his* coming back ?
Have you any hope of it, that you are
getting rid of me so quickly, all of a sudden ?"

" What do you mean ?" she says harshly,
with a shrinking shiver, as if one had torn
open a great gaping wound in her tender
body. " Do you think that if I had had
any hope I should have sent for *you ?* He
is not one to speak lightly, to say one
thing to-day and one to-morrow ; I should
wear out my ears with listening before I
heard the wheels of his carriage coming
back. No, no !" (with a low sobbing sigh)
" I have no hope ! It is humiliating to
speak of hope in such a case, is not it ? I
suppose I should not, if I had any spirit."

 · " If you have really done with him *for*

ever, then," says the young man, in a voice which is still half doubting, " Lenore—I do not want to be glad at what makes you sorry ; but how can I help it ?—then, for God's sake, come to me ; what is there to stand between us ? I *know* I can make you forget him ; even to-day—perhaps you will laugh at me for saying so—you seem to hate me a shade less than you did. Oh, beloved ! out of the great harvest of love that you lavished on him—him who did not care to take it, who hardly stooped to pick it up, who tossed it carelessly back to you— have not you saved *one grain* for me, who have been hungry and famished so long ?"

There are tears in his shaken voice, though none in his eyes ; and indeed a man who *weeps* in wooing mostly damns himself. In a hairy blubbered face there must always be less of the moving than the ridiculous.

" Say ' yes,' " he cries, with a passionate

agony of pleading, twining both his arms once more about her. " I will hold you here until you say it. I will let no sound but 'yes' pass those lips that have never yet given me a kind word or a kiss worth the taking."

" What am I to say 'yes' to ?" she asks, holding aloof from him, as much as may be, with the old gesture of shrinking distaste. " Am I to say that I will marry you ? Well, I said that a month ago ; that is settled. Why must we go over all the old story again ?"

" But *do* we mean the same thing ?" asks Scrope, with distrustful vehemence. " That is the question. Will you marry me *now—at once*, without any senseless, causeless delay ?"

She has drawn herself away from him, and now turns, and walking to the window, looks blankly out on the drear, white, snow world—on the long sharp icicles hanging from the eaves.

" Speak," he says, his voice sharpened and roughened, following her to the other side of the room.   " I am waiting—I will wait on you as long as you please ; but if I keep you here to the Judgment Day I will not go unanswered !   Will you marry me *to-morrow ?*—great Heavens ! if it had not been for this unhappy *contretemps*, by to-morrow you would have been four days my wife !—or will you not ?"

She is trembling all over, and her cold white face is twitched with pain and wet with unwiped tears.

" Not *to-morrow !*" she says, with an involuntary shudder ; " not so soon—not quite so soon.   Let me have time to draw my breath !   I am not well ; as I live I am not well.   See how thin I have grown " (holding out a hand, on which the wandering veins and the small bones indicate their

places more clearly than they did last year).
" I, who " (smiling) " used to be so afraid
of growing too fat! I do not think I need
be afraid of that now, need I ? Let me
get quite well—quite strong first. I shall
be better worth your taking then."

"Lenore!" cries the young man, seizing her
by the arm, in an access of sudden and un-
controllable passion, "did you ever in all your
life think of anyone but yourself ? What
business have you to spoil my life for me ?
What business have you to make me a laugh-
ing-stock for everybody ?—tell me that ?"

" I have no business—none," she answers, drooping her long neck and sobbing.

" Will you marry me *to-morrow*, Lenore ?" (speaking with the stern quiet of
self-constraint).

" Not to-morrow—not to-morrow," she
answers wildly, turning her head restlessly
from side to side. " I meant really to have
married you on Tuesday — you cannot

doubt that ? Had I not my wedding-dress
on ? But see how ill the thought has made
me. Give me six months. In six months
I shall get used to the idea ; perhaps I
shall get the better of my temper. Six
months is a long time ; things that happened six months ago seem a long way
off " (her eyes straying dreamily out to the
still white trees and the square church
tower).

" I see how it is," he says fiercely ; " I
have been very patient with you, and you
think I shall be patient always. You
are mistaken ; I am sick of patience ;
I have done with it. I will marry you *now*
or *never*."

At his words, her swimming eyes flash,
and the wet carnation flowers hotly on her
cheeks.

" Do you wish," she cries, violently, " for
a wife who hates your touch ?—who dreads
being left alone with you ?—who never

hears your footstep without longing to fly out of sight—out of earshot of you ? If you do, you have odd taste !"

He clenches his hands, and his teeth close hard on his under lip, but he does not trust himself to speak.

" Is not it my own interest to be fond of you—to marry you ?" she continues, in strong excitement. " Are not you rich and prosperous ? and have not I all my life been in love with ease and wealth and pleasure ? Is it from choice that I wake all night ? I am sick of being unhappy, and fretting, and hating everybody. God knows I would be happy if I could ! Be patient a little longer—only a little."

But he only answers—" *Now* or *never.*"

" Well, then, it must be *never !*" she answers, vehemently—" there—you have said it yourself; it is *your* doing, not mine. It is *you* who have thrown *me* over—not *I* you."

"Very well," he answers, in a husky whisper, hastily averting his face, to hinder her from seeing the havoc that despair is working on its beauty ; "you are right ; it shall be *never !*"

Utter silence for a space : silence as deep as if they had been dead.

"Lenore," he says at length, turning towards her for the last time his clay-white face and the indignant agony of his eyes, "you make one say ugly things to you. Were you ever anything but a curse to any one that you had to do with ? You have cursed full six months of my life, but you shall curse no more of it : I *will* do without you. There is no lesson so hard that one cannot learn it in time, and I will."

She is silent.

"Even for a good woman, who had loved one, and whom one had lost by death, one would not mourn for ever," he continues.

in the same rough unsteady whisper; "how much less for you, who have never given me anything but unladylike insults—unwomanly gibes! Good-bye, Lenore! Yes, good-bye! But before I go, give me one kiss—one *real* kiss. Since they were to have been *all* mine, spare me one."

So speaking he stoops, and for an instant lays his lips upon her unwilling mouth. Then he goes. Thus she is rid of *all* her lovers.

END OF NOON.

PART III.

NIGHT.

" GOOD night, good sleep, good rest from sorrow,
  To these that shall not have good morrow ;
  Ye gods, be gentle to all these.
  Nay, if death be not, how shall they be ?
  Nay, is there help in heaven ? it may be
  All things and lords of things shall cease."

CHAPTER I.

WHAT THE AUTHOR SAYS.

AFTER Life's little hot day, comes Death's long cool night; whether of the two is the pleasanter? Well, we shall know anon. Oh! patient friends, you have come with me so far, come with me yet a little further. I will not keep you long. Already the shadows stretch themselves; the faint-coloured even cometh. Summer is here again—early summer, early June, as when first, oh reader, you and I met and panted together through the "endless days," when even

night brought not darkness.   Down in
England, the meadows have a lilac tinge
over them, from the ripe heavy-headed
grasses, and the horse-chestnut flower's
spikes have changed into little prickly
green balls.   But we are not in England,
oh reader, you and I ; we are in Switzerland, in the high cold valley of the Engadin.

WHAT JEMIMA SAYS.

We are at the end of our day's journey,
have stiffly descended from the huge dusty
carriage in which we have crampedly sat
all the long and shining day.   To-morrow
we shall reach our final destination, Pontresina.   Meanwhile here we are, up among
the mountains, the torrents, the pines, at
this loveliest village of Bergun.   An hour
has passed since our arrival, and we have
dined, if you can apply that sacred word to
the empty form of tapping with our knives a

black boned chicken's skeleton, and sipping a nauseous wine of the country, black as Tartarus, and with a flavour that is agreeably compounded of pills, slate-pencil, and ink.   There is no denying—degrading as it is to the supremacy of mind over body —that a bad dinner has a depressing effect. Not one of us three but feels cross and empty.   Sylvia tries to sit upon a hard-bottomed, straight-backed chair, as if it were one of her own padded easy ones, and fails.   Lenore stalks to the window and looks over the balcony.   I think that people grow after they are thought grown up, oftener than is usually supposed.   Lenore has certainly grown within the last six months, or perhaps it is only her loss of flesh that gives her such a tall look.   She used to have a good deal of the shapely solidity that constitutes a person's claim to be a fine woman—rather a butcher's term of commendation, at best ;—shapely she

must always be, but *fine* she is no longer;
only very slender and willowy. I pick up
the visitors' book, read the dreary wag-
geries, the lame rhymes, the consequential
commendations of bed and board. I come
to the last entry :

" Mr. Tomkins, London.
" Mrs. Tomkins,   „
" Miss Tomkins,   „
" Miss L. Tomkins, „
" Mr. J. T. Tomkins, „
" Miss Harris,   „

" Exceedingly pleased with the accom-
modation at this hotel—the attendance
excellent, rooms most clean, and food
better than at any other hotel in the
Engadin."

I read this aloud. " There is a prospect for us!"

" You are not serious ? " cries Sylvia,

starting upright in her chair, and opening
eyes as round as marbles in unaffected dis-
may. " That is not *really* there ! You
are only joking !"

" Read for yourself," I answer, handing
the book to her, while I joined our junior
in the window. Well, one must send all
appetite to one's eyes; there is at least
plenty of food for them. The pearly evening sky, cut by the cold lilac peaks ; the
mountains, that wear always round their
waist and feet a girdle of great pines ;
a sombre army—rising, pointed top above
pointed top, in their endless fadeless
green ; the rough torrent course, that fur-
rows the hill's face, like the traces of a
tearful agony ; an evening glimmer of
meadow flowers ; a flash of bright water.
And right under us the little village street,
the deep-roofed low houses, the tiny casements, out of which the lavish pinks and
flowered picotees are hanging ; the queer

sententious inscription on the *chalet* nearest
us :—

> " DAS HAUS STET IN GOTTES HAND,
>   JAN PEDER GRIGORI
>   BIN ICH GENAND."

And is not that Jan Peder himself, sitting
outside, on a log of wood ?   He is old and
withered, and very much the worse for
wear.

Insensibly I begin to forget the void
feeling that ruffled my temper five minutes
ago, as I listen to the soothing drip, drip,
of the two-spouted pump, that is always
pouring into a wooden trough.   The pump
seems to be the rendezvous of the village ;
the leisurely chatter, in this odd mongrel
Romansch tongue, rises soft and subdued
to our ears.   A tinkling of slow bells, as
a herd of lovely smoke-coloured cows come
slowly treading down the street, and stoop
their sleek necks to drink.   If one could

see the inside of these folks' lives no doubt one would find that they were as basely grovelling as those of our own lower orders —lives probably brightened only by garlic and beer; but looking now at the outside of them, on this quiet purple evening, it seems as if one had come upon a little sudden patch of old-world innocent Arcadia.

"I wish that Jan Peder Gregori would go indoors," says Lenore, gravely; "it must be very bad for him, being out so late."

"There must be some one here beside us," I say, leaning over the balcony, and pointing to a second and smaller dusty carriage, drawn up behind our great lumbering ark.

"A man, too," says Lenore, with lazy interest, "if a portmanteau be a sufficient proof of masculinity."

"It is such a bran-new one, too," continue I, laughing, " that he must be either a just-married man, or a man just about to be married."

" Who was it said that a new flannel petticoat was an infallible sign of a bride ?" asks Lenore, languidly. " Does the same hold good of men and portmanteaus ? I wish we could see his initials, but the hat-box hides them.

" Now that I think of it," I say, medita-tively, " I have a vision of having seen vestiges of food on that table in the corner; let us make Kolb find out who he is, for by his luggage, I feel sure that he is an Englishman."

I am right. An Englishman he is, name unknown ; he has come down from St. Moritz, and is on his homeward road ; he is to set off at cock-crow to-morrow, and he went out walking only five minutes before our arrival. This is all the inform-ation we obtain, all the food we get to keep alive our faint and flagging interest.

" Do you mean to stay fustily indoors all evening ?" asks Lenore, presently, with a yawn, " because I do not. I am sick of Jan Peder, and the pump, and the goats ; I shall go and *explore*, like Mrs. Elton in ' Emma.' "

" Do not !" cry I, hastily and dissuasively. " You know that going out when the dew is falling always brings on your cough."

" Pooh !" replies she, lightly. " What matter if it does ? I am going to set up such a stock of strength at Pontresina that it would be a thousand pities not to be a little worse before I get there."

" At least put on your " —— I begin, but she interrupts me.

" Did you ever know me to take advice in all your life ?" she asks, with a petulant gesture. " I should not wonder if I met

our unknown friend of the new portmanteau ; I am not sure that I am not going
to look for him. *Au revoir !"*

I gaze after her and sigh, with a line of
'Elaine' running in my head—

"Being so very wilful, you must go."

CHAPTER II.

"There cannot be a pinch in death more sharp than this is."

WHAT THE AUTHOR SAYS.

AFTER all she puts a shawl over her head; it is not a very thick one, but neither is the mountain air very keen on this softly-creeping summer night. It is red, and the old men and the women sitting in the doorways of the dark little houses stare at it admiringly. She passes amongst them quickly—past the rickety little wooden balconies, the piles of firewood, the numberless odd little

casements, like windows in a doll's house
—it is not *them* that she wants—till, at a
sudden turn, the village is behind her, out
of sight—the laughing, leisurely, chattering
village—and the river that she sought is
before her.   A great bold hill-shoulder
rises in front of her against the dark night-
sky, and beside her the river boils and
maddens along in riotous white play; it is
so swift that the eye cannot follow it; it
tosses high its cold spray, and cries, exult-
ingly, " Oh, snow ! I am as white as you."
Nobody sees her—she is all alone; even
the broad-faced moon has not yet looked
in silver and pearl over the hill. When
one is alone one does many foolish things.
Lenore throws herself on her knees on a
flat stone close to the brink—dashed, indeed, by the stream's stormy white dust—
and speaks out loud to it :

   " Oh, good, kind little river ! will you

drown memory for me ?—will you drown Paul ?"

Lenore is not always thinking of Paul ; sometimes for almost a day she forgets him ; but, long as it is since he cast her off, and short as was the time during which she possessed him, the impulse still holds her, on seeing any beautiful thing, to say, " I will show it to Paul ;" on hearing any witty thing, " I will tell it to Paul." Paul was a cross fellow, cruel and cold, as she sometimes tells herself ; but he would have loved this mad river, biting and ravening with fierce foam-teeth against the dark boulders that lie in its bed, and crying violently to them, " Let me pass !" If he were here now, among the yellow trefoil, his arm round her waist and her head on his shoulder !—they two standing, in a dumb ecstasy, with only the larches waving their green plumes above their heads, and the water's endless restless roar, that ceases

not day nor night, January nor June,
making a loud hubbub at their feet—alone
with the river, the mountains, and God !
She can almost feel his arm ; she turns her
eyes to look up into his, but then the
dream flies ; there are no kind eyes to look
into—there is no Paul—none !

She starts up hastily, and hurries on.
The gorge narrows ; there is only room for
her and for the river—the panting fury of
the stream.   "Oh river ! you take my
breath away.   Tarry a little; I cannot
keep up with you !"   But the river makes
answer : " I cannot tarry ; I have an errand
into the great grey sea."   On and on, on
and on she saunters, not heeding how far
nor whither, until at length she comes to a
slight hand-bridge of planks, that gives
and vibrates beneath her.   There she
stands, and leans over the slender railing,
gazing, with eyes that try in vain to keep
up with it, at the swirling torrent.   The

evening is both darkening and lightening :
darkening, for the sun is gone further and
further away ; lightening, for the moon is
coming — yea, come. Already she has
washed the hills' faces with her cool silver
flood : now her pearl-white feet have
reached — have lightly trodden on the
water—the wonderful water ! Can it be
all the same—the same when it lies in
opal sleep, and when it plunges against
and angrily smites its drenched rocks ? If
one had but some one—some dear person
—to show it all to !

After crossing the bridge the path she
has hitherto followed takes a sharp turning
round the spur of a hill, and is immediately
lost to sight. As she stands, still leaning
over the rickety hand-rail, and watching
the moon-coloured bubbles, she hears a
footstep coming along this unseen path. It
is growing late ; the moon is rising high ;
this place is inconceivably lonely. Her

first impulse is to turn and run homewards,
but her second contradicts it. Why should
she stir ? Bah ! it is probably some innocent rough peasant, clumping home to bed
in his deep-eaved *chalet*. He will stare
at her cloak, and probably give her a
Romansch " good-night," to which she will
be puzzled to respond; so she stays.
Nearer and nearer comes the footstep, and
her heart beats a trifle quicker than its
wont. Her eyes are fixed on the corner
which will give to view the owner of this
slow and intermittent tread. Here he
comes, out of the rock-shadow into the
light ! He is not a peasant ! He is—
surely, he is an Englishman ! He is—
Paul ! Oh, God in heaven ! it cannot be !
Men dress so much alike—there is such a
deceptive resemblance between all the men
of a class at a little distance. He comes
a step or two nearer, then stops and looks
upwards. The moon shines down full and

white on his upturned face—the honest,
shrewd face, that is neither gentle nor
beautiful. She sees his cool calm eyes
glitter in the moonbeams. He is carelessly
dressed, without any necktie. His strong
throat rises bare and muscular, and his
hands are buried deep in the pockets of
the old Dinan shooting jacket. Do you
think that she faints or topples over into
the water, or screams or laughs hysterically,
or calls out loud ? Not she! She only
stands still, with one slight hand hard
grasping the hand-rail, and with a heart
whose loud pulsations drown the voice of
the triumphant foamy stream, waiting for
her heaven to come to her. Has Death
let her slip by him, having seen her bitter
pain ? Is she already in the blessed
land ? Paul is so busy moon-gazing
that he is close to her—his foot is upon
the plank — before he perceives her.
Then he jumps almost out of his clothes

—out of his Dinan shooting jacket—out of his skin.

" Lenore ! ! !"

She could not have cried " *Paul!*" in answer if you had offered her all the kingdoms of the world as a bribe. He stoops his tall head till his eager face is close to hers ; he stares hard into her eyes ; he even stretches out his hand and touches her red cloak to assure himself that she is real. Yes, it is no ghost-woman ; it is a real Lenore, with a face much paler, indeed, than the Lenore he remembers—a face grave with the gravity of intense emotion, touched with the trouble of overpowering wonder—that is looking back at him with wide and lovely eyes.

" God Almighty ! who would have thought of seeing *you* here ?"

In the accents of intense surprise it is difficult to ascertain the presence or absence of joy or sorrow. One would be puzzled to say whether Paul were very glad or very grieved at this meeting at the world's end with his old love.

" Lenore !—*is it Lenore?*" (again narrowly scanning her white and quivering face.) " How, in the name of wonder, did you come here ?"

It is stupid to be so tongueless, is not it ?—standing dumb, with hanging head, like a child playing at being shy. But she seems to have lost the art of framing words.

" Will not you speak to me ?" he continues, with an eager hesitation, mistaking the cause of her speechlessness ; " will not you shake hands with me ?"

She puts out her hand in a moment : does he feel how it is shaking as it lies in his cool clasp ?

" You—you—are not *alone* here ?" (involuntarily glancing at her left hand). " You are with—with "——

"No, I am not alone," she answers, speaking every word very slowly and carefully, as if not quite sure whether the right words would come; "Jemima and Sylvia "——

"*Jemima!*" he says, pronouncing the word with a lingering emphasis, as if it carried him back into memory, and smiling rather pensively.

Both are silent for a few moments ;—only two voices are heard : the river's loud hoarse one, as it keeps calling always to the rocks and the dumb green pines, and the grasshopper's sharp and shrill—and infinitely content. If it could but last for ever ! They two standing on that narrow bridge, on a sheet of silver, the river—all silver, too—tearing and roaring below them ; the larches softly tossing their small green feathers ; the unsleeping grasshopper singing his pleasant song ; and they two looking kindly into each other's eyes.

But when could one ever say to any happy moment, as Joshua said to the docile sun, "Stand thou still"? He will not stand still; he could not if he would; he is jostled away by his pushing younger brothers.

"How often I have wondered whether I should ever meet you again," says Paul, presently, with a long sigh; "after all, the world is small—and if I did, where and how? Certainly, this is the last place that ever would have entered my head; and yet, only five minutes ago I was thinking of you."

"Were you?" she says, softly, while her eyes shine gently back at him, like beautifullest dew-wet flowers through happy tears!

"You have forgiven me?" he says, anxiously catching hold of her other hand, and holding both in the same loose friendly clasp in which he had before held the one. "We are friends, are not we? At peace?"

She has no hands to hide her face; she
cannot hinder him from seeing how her
drooped eyes brim over—how the heavy
great tears are rolling down over her
smart scarlet cloak. In the tender gentleness of her small wet face there is not
much war.

"Do not cry," he says, looking surprised
and miserable, as a man always does, when
a woman unexpectedly weeps. "What is
there to cry about? I am not" (smiling
rather awkwardly) "going to scold you,
this time. You know I always was a good
hand at lecturing, was not I? Often and
often since I have wished that I had not
been quite such a good one. . . . I can
hardly believe that it *is* you," he says, after
a pause, again interrupting the river's and
the grasshopers' duet. "What have you
been doing to yourself? Somehow you
are different. You are too old to grow, I
suppose; people do not grow at nineteen;

but—but—surely you are thinner than you used to be ? Have you been ill ? Are you ill now ?"

" Not very," she answers, lightly, " anybody else would have made a trifle of it, but you know I always make the most of things, and I have not much of a constitution—so they tell me."

He does not ask any other question for the moment.

" For my part, I am glad," she continues, with a restless laugh. " I never could see what use a good constitution was to anyone, except to make them suffer more, and die harder when their time came."

" I suppose you have been threatening to break a bloodvessel again," he says, with a smiling allusion to what she had told him on one of the earliest days of their acquaintance. " Good God ! can that be only a year ago ?"

" Only a year ago !" she echoes, dreamily. " But a year is a long time."

" You are pale, too," he says, proceeding with his scrutiny; "are you always pale now ? The only time that I remember you as pale as you are now was that night when I upset you into the Rance ! How wet you were ! How the water dripped from your long hair ! I did not believe till then that women really *had* such long hair. I can see you now !" His grey eyes look kind and almost wistful as he thus travels back into the pretty dead past.

" Can you ?" she says, almost inaudibly.

" It was all a mistake, I suppose," he continues, sighing, "a blunder—a bungle— but it was pleasant while it lasted, was not it ?"

She cannot speak for tears.

" Lenore," he says, after another silence, in a tone of stronger excitement than any that he has yet used, ." I am going to tell

you something. Often and often I have
wondered whether I should ever have the
chance of telling you. Sometimes I have
wished that I should, and sometimes I have
hoped that I should not. It does not much
matter what you think of me now, one way
or another, but I do not think that it will
improve your opinion of either my wisdom
or my humility. Do you remember that
last letter you sent me?"

She is not pale now; he cannot accuse
her of it. No rose in any midsummer
garden was ever so red; and her streaming
eyes flash in the mild moonlight with the
old angry spirit. Is he going to twit her
with that poor little overture that mis-
carried so piteously?

"I did not believe in it," he goes on,
still in hot excitement. "I was sore and
mad from your galling bitter words. Lenore" (almost entreatingly), "why do you
let your tongue cut like a knife? I thought

it was only a flirting manœuvre to get me back and make a fool of me a second time. I hate being made a fool of! Nobody had ever taken the trouble to do it before. I hate being trodden upon. I like to walk upright and go my own way."

" Well ?"

" You remember the answer I sent—I hope you burnt it—I am not proud of it," reddening through all his sun tan. " Well, when it was gone I read your letter over again, and by dint of poring over it line by line I grew to think that there was a true ring in it. Lenore, it was very clever of you ! I do not know how you managed to get that true ring. I began to think of— of—the dear old time " (his voice, though he is a man, shakes a little). " I began— you will laugh at me for thinking of such a trifle at such a moment—to remember the old blue gown and Huelgoat."

She turns away, and leans over the

bridge ; and, unseen by him, unseen by anyone, her tears hotly drop into the cold river and are swallowed by it.

" I recollected things you used to say," he continues, with a pensive smile, given rather to the past than the present. " You had such a pretty fond way of saying things—well" (dashing his hand across his forehead, and abruptly changing his tone) "the upshot of it was that I resolved to ask you to—to—to—kiss and make friends in short—I suppose one may as well word it in that childish way as any other. I had even " (beginning to laugh harshly, for one's laughs at one's own expense are rarely melodious) "got a new pen, squared my elbows, and sat down to write to you." She is trembling all over, and panting, as one breathless from a long race.

" Why did not you ?—why did not you ?" she cries, with almost a wail.

"*Why did not I?*" he repeats, looking at her with unfeigned astonishment. "I wonder at your asking that. Why? Because at that very moment, not a week after you had composed that triumph of pathos" (with a bitter sneer), "I heard of your engagement to Scrope. I saw how much the *true ring* was worth then; I believe I laughed. There is always something to be thankful for, and I was heartily thankful that I had not written. There is no use in eating more dirt than one can help in this world, is there?"

"But I am not engaged now!" she cries, passionately. "I can hardly believe that I ever was really; people exaggerate things so in the telling. I think it was always more play than earnest."

"*More play than earnest!*" he repeats, in utter and blank astonishment. "Why, I understood that the wedding day had come—that you were all dressed—and that it was only put off on account of your having been taken suddenly ill !"

" Yes," she answers, incoherently ; " thank God, I was ill, very ill ; that was what saved me ! Thank God ! Thank God !"

" *Saved* you !" he repeats, looking at her with unlimited wonder. " How do you mean ? Surely it was your own doing ? It was only put off, was not it ?—it is still to be ?"

" Never ! never !" she cries, wildly. " Who can have told you such things ? It was all a farce from beginning to end ; it never was anything serious. I—I— think I must have been a little off my head."

" And you are not engaged to Scrope ?" (with an accent of extreme surprise).

" Not I," she answers, vehemently ; " do not suggest anything so dreadful."

" Nor to any one else ?"

"*Any one else !*" she echoes, scornfully. " To whom else should I be ? Must I always be engaged to some one ?"

Now that it is all clear between them, now that all clouds of misconception have been swept away, now that they are all alone here in the moonlight, surely he will take her in his arms.   Her head will rest on the shoulder of the old jacket, where it has so often confidently lain before.   But he only turns away with something like a curse, and says, half under his breath, " God ! what lies people tell !"   A silence. When next Paul speaks it is in a con- .strained and sedulously governed voice.

" I did not bless either you or him that day, I can tell you—not that *that* did you much harm ; but this was quite at the first, quite.   When a thing has sense and justice in it one soon gives up kicking against it. I have long given up kicking against this ; I have grown so wise " (laughing,

nervously) "that I acquiesce in it contentedly."

"Do you?" she says, and her throat
seems to have grown suddenly dry, and to
send forth only harsh and ugly sounds.

"Perhaps — perhaps — you will come
round to him yet," says Paul, speaking
with a very white face, and a tremor in his
deep voice, "in time, you know; time does
surprising things—things that one would
not believe! You — you — might do
worse."

A fiery searing pain goes through her
heart.

"You are very good," she says, while.
the flame of her hot eyes dries her tears,
"but I really do not see what business it is
of yours."

"None," he answers, almost humbly;
"none! I beg your pardon for having
said it, but you know you consented just
now that we should be friends, and friends

may take an interest in each other's future, may not they ?"

She does not answer ; she is listening to the grasshopper — his sharp treble song seems to have grown very dismal all of a sudden.

" Lenore," cries the other, impulsively, again catching her small hands, " before we say anything more, let me tell you—I *must* tell you—about—about—my future."

" Well ?"

Her eyes, dry now, achingly dry, are staring back at him, wild with an unnamed fear.

" My people have been up at St. Moritz," he says, going on rapidly with his story, "so have I, for the last two months ; I am hurrying home now as fast as I can, to get things straight.   I am going—perhaps you have heard it already—I am going to be married."

When one receives a mortal blow, some-

times one does not feel much pain at the
first—so they tell me ; one is only stunned.
I do not think that Lenore feels much pain,
only her wits go a woolgathering. Not
for long, however. Even though one is
lightheaded from extremest agony, one has
still the womanly instinct to draw a decent
cloak over one's ugly yawning wounds.
Not much more than the usual interval
between question and answer has elapsed,
before some one—some kind spirit, I think,
who has crept inside her cold and quivering
body—speaks in almost Lenore's voice—
speaks with a stiff little smile :

" To your cousin ?"

" Yes, to my cousin."

A little trifling pause, that would not be
noticed, so short is it, in any ordinary conversation ; a pause, during which Lenore
is fighting more fiercely than ever the
typical lioness fought for her whelps—
fighting for a voice, for a laugh, for civil

careless words ; and he or she who in one of these mortal battles fights strongly, with heart and soul, with decency and self-respect on his or her side, mostly over-comes.   Only it takes a great deal of lint to heal the wounds afterwards.   Lenore overcomes.   But the victory is hardly com-plete ; she cannot let him see her face. She leans over the bridge side, as she leant five minutes ago to hide her happy tears ; but there are no tears to hide now.

" The ideal girl !" she says, with a sort of laugh.   " The woman with eyes like a shot partridge's — rather dull, but very loving !   You see I remember all about her."

Paul does not speak ; he also leans over the bridge, and there is not much of the triumphant bridegroom in the eyes that are idly fixed on a pointed rock, grey, and shining with wet moonbeams, which every minute the stream deluges.

"If you remember, I always prophesied it," says the girl, feeling her words come more readily; "only, like Cassandra, nobody believed my prophecies."

"Why did you prophesy it?" he asks almost angrily. "There was no sense in such a prophecy—no ground for it. There was not such a thought in anyone's head— no, nor ever would have——"

He stops suddenly. She does not speak, only she shakes her head gently. Her wits have come quite back; she has buried the pain in a shallow hole, out of sight, for the moment. When this is over—when he is gone—it will shake off the light covering of its temporary grave, and rise up like a giant. Then again she will have to fight; but now for the moment she has won a most numb quiet.

"Why do you shake your head?" he asks abruptly. "Does it mean that you do not believe me? At least in the old time you used to give me credit for speaking truth—sometimes too much truth to please you; why should I deceive you now?—*now* that no word that either you or I could speak could bring us one jot nearer each other?"

Still she only leans her arms on the rail of the bridge—leans heavily on it—and her drooped head sinks low down.

"When was it that you prophesied it?" he asks almost in a whisper, coming nearer her. "Was it at Huelgoat, or at Chateaubriand's tomb, as we stood and watched the waves and the seagulls? If you did, I compliment you; you were indeed far-seeing." (No answer.) "I never was one to care violently for anybody—never. The game never seemed to me worth the candle. It does not sound well, but I had always liked myself best; but—somehow I like to say it now, though there is not much sense in it (shake your head as much

as you please)—but, before God, I did care
for you beyond measure in my way—it was
not a very pleasant way—only I tried my
best to hide it. I knew your amiable peculiarity of never valuing what you could get ;
but I *did* love you—I did—I *did !*" (rising
into an emphasis and excitement most unlike him as he ends).

"Did you," she says faintly, a little
spark of animation coming into her face
and into her dull eyes. "I thought you
liked me ; afterwards they all said you did
not."

"Well, I love no one beyond measure
now, I suppose," he says hastily, pushing
the hair off his forehead with a cross and
jerky movement. "My affections are quite
within bounds—well in hand" (smiling
ironically). "The other was the pleasant-
est while it lasted, but no doubt this is the
healthier state." (Still silence.) "It is
much better as it is," he says presently,

speaking vehemently, and as if more with
a view to convincing himself than her.
" If we had married then, how we should
have hated each other by now ! Did we
ever look at anything from the same point
of view ?—and you are not a woman to be
shaped to a husband's liking. Good God !
how I laughed at that idiot West's notion
of *moulding* you ! You would not have
given in, neither should I. Yes, we should
have been miserable."

" Miserable—yes, miserable—*most* miserable," she echoes very slowly and mechanically ; but whether she applies the
word to the hypothetical case he puts, or
to her own actual one, is not clear even to
herself.

" You agree with me ?" he says sharply,
as if not much gratified by the discovery
of her acquiescence. " Of course ! I knew
you did. Yes, it is better for both of us ;
specially better for *you*."

" Much better," she says, speaking with an immense effort, and even accomplishing a laugh. " As you say, when did we ever look at anything from the same point of view, even during the short time we were together ?—how short ! how short !" (uttering the words in a dragging, dreary way.) " Hardly a day passed that we did not quarrel. Yes, it was pleasant at the time —*quite* pleasant. I suppose that your— your—cousin " (with a tight, strained smile) " will not mind my allowing *that*, will she ? But no doubt we shall both do better—I, as you say, especially."

A little pause.

" Do you remember," he says suddenly, " that day at St. Malo ; how I "—

She interrupts. " I remember nothing," she says firmly, though her pale lips tremble. " I have the worst memory in the world." He looks mortified, and relapses into silence. " Tell me," she says presently, with a nervous excitement in her manner, " tell me all about *yourself ;* that is much more interesting. When is it to be—what day exactly ? I should like to think of you, you know—to drink your health, and " (laughing hysterically) " I suppose I ought to send you a present, ought not I ?"

" For God's sake, do not !" he cries hastily, " unless you can send me your bad memory ; I *should* thank you for that."

" You *never* quarrel with her, I suppose?" continues the girl, drawing strength even from the very intensity of her own misery to speak collectedly, and even smilingly. " It is all smooth sailing, like a boat on a duck-pond ! No doubt you can *mould* her, like a piece of clay, into whatever shape you like."

Paul reddens. " She is a good girl," he says moodily ; " and when I am away from you I know that I shall be happy with her

—at least" (sighing heavily) " I ought to be ; at all events, I shall have peace—that is something. All my life before I met you I thought it was everything." (After a pause) " Thank God she does not know how to sneer."

" And when is it to be ?" she asks, still smiling ; "you know you have not told me ; tell me. I wish to know the day— the very day."

" Immediately," he says, feverishly ; "the sooner the better. What is there to wait for ?"

" Well, I will think of you," she says, commanding her voice with great difficulty, and stretching out her trembling hand kindly to him ; "yes, I will—that is " (breaking into an unsteady laugh), " if—if —I do not forget."

" Do nothing of the kind," he cries, roughly pressing the slender cold fingers ; "neither *then* nor *ever !* Let us make a compact, never to think of each other again. What pleasant thoughts can we have of one another? Least of all, think of me on that day," he continues after an interval, speaking with the signs of strong excitement. "I ask it of you as a favour; if your face comes between me and the parson" (laughing harshly) "I shall not be very ready with my responses! Let me have one good look at you!" (after another pause, while his breath comes quick and short) "just one. It would be a pity quite to forget the face of the handsomest woman one ever knew, would not it? There!— There!" There is the pallor of a mad longing on his cold shrewd face, as he stands staring and stammering in the moonlight. "Good-bye, lovely eyes!" he says, in a hoarse whisper; "good-bye, lovely lips! you gave me no peace while I had you; but, yet I wish—oh God! how I wish——"

He stops abruptly. His mad fond words have brought back the solace of all the sorrowful to her smarting eyes; they are shining with the soft dimness of tendeɪ tears, as they grow to his harsh and altered face.

"Wish nothing," she says, gently. "I have wished many things in my time—that you were dead; that I myself were; that one could have things twice over, or not at all—but you see they have none of them come true."

"Let me, at least, wish one thing," he cries, violently. "Whether you let me, or no, I *will* wish it! I will pray, and urgently entreat God for it—that this—this *hell*, that is just half a step off heaven, may not come over again! Lenore, pretty Lenore, what ill-luck makes us both live in England? What security have we that we shall not come across each other again, and yet again, and yet again?"

" There is not much danger," she says, calmly, " at least, not yet awhile : we are not going home ; we are going up to Pontresina for many months—for all the summer."

"To Pontresina ?" he exclaims, brusquely. " What are you going there for ? Health or pleasure ? Not *health* surely ?" peering at her again with an anxious suspicion.

" Partly," she answers ; and then trying to speak lightly and merrily, " I suppose being over-lively and over-amused wears one out as much as over-work or over-grief ; I was so gay last winter—so gay— that I danced all the flesh off my bones."

He makes no comment on this announcement.

" I am going to lay up such a store of strength against next winter," she continues, laughing almost loudly, " for I mean to be gayer than ever then—gayer than ever."

The contrast between the words she is

uttering and the black devastation that is laying waste her soul, strikes her with such bitter force that she turns away sharply.

"Do you?" he says, fiercely. "I dare say! What is it to me? Why do you tell me?"

Higher and higher the fair broad moon has been sailing; she has reached her zenith; now, nothing escapes her; every larch feather, every yeasty crown of froth, every daisy and fine grass blade, she has daintly washed.

"I am going," Paul says, with rough suddenness. "What am I waiting for? Can you tell me that? If I stayed here all to-night and to-morrow, and the night after, what would be changed? This vile stream would still be thundering on, and we should still be standing here, eating our hearts out with longing for things that, if we had them, would not give us content."

"Yes," she says, and her own pretty

womanly voice is almost as harsh as his,
" go ! Who is keeping you ?"

His face is white—so white—with the
pallor of unwilling passion, and he is
trembling all over. "And must I leave
you here, all alone in this desolate place ?"
he asks, in a husky whisper ; "all alone, as
I found you ?"

And she echoes, " All alone !"

" You are not frightened ?"

Again she laughs, though the muscles
about her face seem tight and stiff. "What
should I be frightened at ?"

Their hands are interlocked, and their
eyes are fixed on each other's faces.

"This is the third time we have said
'Good-bye,'" he says, indistinctly. " The
last was bad enough, but, for my part, I
liked it better than this ; and the first—
Lenore, do you remember the first on the
steamboat at St. Malo ?"

" I remember *nothing*," she says, breaking out into impetuous passion, while the blood runs headlong to her cheeks. " How many times must I tell you that it is an *accursed* word ? I have torn it out of my vocabulary ! I always look on—*on*—now" (speaking feverishly). " Surely there must be something pleasant ahead somewhere— somewhere !"

" Perhaps," he says, gloomily ; "but one thing I am sure of—oh Lenore, you are sure of it, too—and that is, that there is nothing so pleasant ahead as what we have left behind !"

These are his last words.

CHAPTER III.

WHAT JEMIMA SAYS.

AND now we have done with Bergun; in all probability we shall
see its little eaves and deep doll's-
house windows never again. How happily
might one (one is not equivalent to *I* here)
spend a honeymoon among its rocks, and
pine-slopes, and flowered fields, always
supposing that one had brought one's own
food with one. I confess to an opinion
that the chicken's black skeleton, and the
untold nauseousness of the Sasseila, would
cool the ardour of the warmest pair that

ever yawned and fondled through the conventional month. We are still, however, in the foodless land of the Engadin; we have reached Pontresina. It is a long name is not it? But the name is longer than the place; it is only a cluster of houses, white as the defacer of all beauty, whitewash, can make them. If I had the world's reins in my hand I would have put him that invented whitewash to even a feller death than that which I would have inflicted on the twin demons who brought up gunpowder and electricity from hell's lowest pit. At the foot of a long stern hill the village humbly crouches, while round it stand a silent solemn conclave of great mountains—white snow spires reaching heavenwards—God's church steeples; while far off, a grey-green glacier dimly shines. Oh, mighty mountains, you coldly awe me with your

"aloof and loveless permanence."

The trees cluster in the valley, but the great hills stand bare-headed before God. Here we are at the little hotel '*De la Croix Blanche*,' having taken root among the whitewash. We have been here a week, and we have yawned a good deal. The season has hardly begun—at least for the English—and it has rained an infinity. We have even had the doubtful pleasure of seeing flakes of unseasonable snow. There are no books to be got, and we have exhausted our few Tauchnitz novels. To-day we have grown tired of our own sitting-room, and have strayed objectlessly up to the general *salon* at the top of the house. It is a bare light room, white-washed, of course. A carpet would be pleasant to-day, but no rag of carpet is there; only aggressively clean squares of deal, intersected with red pine. There has been a wedding party in the house all day; their all-pervading din and to us incomprehensible Romansch mirth have had a large share in driving us upwards. It is afternoon now, and, thank God, they are gone. We have been standing out in the balcony, watching their departure, as they pack themselves into their shabby hooded carriages, garlanded with dusty green wreaths. Yes, they are gone; the arm of each gawky youth, with ostentatious candour, clasping the solid waist of his maiden. Now that they are gone, Sylvia retires inside, grumbling and shivering.

" Had not you better go in too ?" I say to Lenore; "it is very damp. You will never get well if you do not take more care of yourself."

" Why *should* I get well ?" she says, querulously. " I do not want to get well; what object in life should I have if I were well ? Being ill is something to do. I can be interested in my symptoms and

my tonics ; I would not be well for
worlds."

I look at her compassionately—at her
sharpened profile ; it is getting a look of
pinched and suffering discontent.   Where
is its lovely debonair roundness ?   Alas !
even since we left Bergun it has been slipping—oh, how quickly !—away.

"You may get me a shawl if you like,"
she says, presently, "and a chair."

I re-enter the *salon* to fetch them.
Sylvia is sitting with the landlord's book of
dried plants before her, lamentably turning
over the leaves.   At the best of times nothing can be more melancholy than a dried
flower—a colourless skeleton, without any
likeness to itself.   One ought to be in the
best of spirits to look at such a collection
as is now engaging Mrs. Prodger's slack
attention.   I return with the shawl—a
heavy and warm one—and wrap it about
my youngest sister, and then remain by

her side, vacantly gazing at the view.
The rain has ceased, but the clouds still
hide the top of the glacier mountain; one
tiny cloudlet has lost its way, and is wandering about near the hill foot, slowly
evaporating, and losing its thin life. The
balcony where we are is much higher than
the opposite houses; it can look magni-
ficently down on their roofs. They are a
queer little row; not in a line at all, but
each seeming to be shoving and elbowing
its neighbour, in order to get forwardest;
in the narrow street below, a man is leaning against a doorpost, smoking a long
pipe; another is sweeping the round stones
of the pavement with a besom. How can
one possibly get up any interest in either
of them.

"I do not think Kolb behaved quite
honestly about this place," says Sylvia's
voice, dolorously, from the interior; "somehow one never can get foreigners to speak

quite the truth—he certainly told me distinctly, when I asked him, that one might always wear *demi-saison* dresses here."

We are both too much depressed to join even in abuse of Kolb's mendacity. Several more leaves turned over; a heavy sigh.

" I wish the Websters were here; they talked of going abroad this summer. I will write and advise them to come here."

" Rather a case of the fox that had lost his tail," I say, laughing dismally.

" Tell them not to bring any *demi-saison* dresses," subjoins Lenore, sarcastically.

Several moments of forlorn silence. Sylvia has finished her book, and with a vague and mistaken idea that we have got some little piece of amusement that we are privately *worrying* without giving her information of it, she issues forth a second time and joins us. We are all in a row, like three storks standing on one leg on a housetop. The cloudlet has quite melted; there is not a trace of it. I wish I could melt too. The man has stopped sweeping. Suddenly—no, not suddenly—gradually a sound of distant wheels and bells salutes our ears. A vehicle of some kind is approaching at a brisk trot from the direction of Samaden.

"Coming *here*, do you think?" I say, with a spark of animation shooting, as I feel, from my lack-lustre eye.

"No such luck," answers Lenore, gloomily.

"No doubt it is going on to 'The Krone,'" says Sylvia, peevishly. "Everybody goes to 'The Krone.' I wish we had gone there. It was all Kolb's doing."

The bells ring louder, the horses' hoofs stamp the stones more distinctly; it is in sight. Yes, a carriage, twin brother to our own late one, only that it is shut on account of the weather; four horses, piles of luggage, dusty tarpaulin. A moment of breathless suspense; we all lean over the balcony as far as our necks and heads will take us. Yes!—no!—yes! Far down in the street, right under our eager eyes, it is pulling up.

"My heart was in my mouth!" says Lenore, smiling a broad smile of relief. "I thought it *was* going on to 'The Krone.'"

"We are too high up here," I say, excitedly; "we should see better from our own windows."

Hereupon we all rush violently, helter-skelter, downstairs to our sitting-room, which is on a lower floor. Only one window gives upon the street; it is small, but we all huddle into it. M. Enderlin, the landlord, letting down the steps; Madame Enderlin courtseying; Marie and

Menga hovering near, ready to carry out parcels.

"*Maid*, of course," I say, as the first occupant slowly emerges. "She looks rather wet; evidently she was in the *coupé* with the courier, and they only took her inside because it rained."

A man's legs and a wideawake, then a great deal of golden hair and a plump smart woman's figure. Being above them, we see none of their faces.

"Nothing looks so nice for travelling as those French lawns trimmed with un-bleached Cluny," says Sylvia, with pensive envy; "they never show the dust."

"Bride and bridegroom," say I. "What a bore! They will not do us much good; they will be swallowed up in one an-other."

"They look like *people*, however," says Sylvia, by which expression she means to intimate a favourable opinion of the new-

comers' gentility. " If they are nice," she
continues, " I mean, really people that one
would like to know—and Kolb could
easily find out that—we might make a party
to go up Piz Languard with them."

" There is some one else with them,"
cry I, eagerly. " Surely they cannot
have taken their parents to *chaperone*
them !"

" Like the people at Dinan," says
Lenore, drily, " who went a wedding tour
à l'anglaise, and took the bride's mother
and the bridegroom's with them."

A fat but nicely-booted female foot
slowly treads the step, and then the
ground ; it and its fellow support a form of
shapely mature portliness. Having descended, this last figure lifts its face to look
at the little cross swinging out as the inn
sign in the street.

" Good heavens !" cries Lenore, emphatically.

"Why that pious ejaculation?" say I gaily, my spirits having gone up fifty per cent. at the prospect of human companionship.

" Did not you see?" breaks out Lenore excitedly. " Do not you know who they are?"

" Not I. How should I?"

" Why, old Mrs. Scrope, to be sure— Charlie's mother."

" What! all three of them?" I say derisively. " My dear child, you are dreaming."

" Impossible!" says Sylvia, straining her little neck out of window to catch a last glimpse ; but they are gone. " You have such a mania for seeing likenesses that no one else can. How could you tell? one only saw their backs."

" And should not I know my own mother-in-law's back among a hundred?" says Lenore, with sardonic mirth.

"Oh, if it was only her back," I say, with a sigh of relief, "I do not mind; all old women's backs are much alike."

"Are they ?" says Lenore, with a grim smile. "I do not agree with you; there are backs and backs; but I do not confine myself to backs—I saw her *face*, and my ex-mother-in-law's it was, I am sorry to say."

"And the other two were the married daughter and her husband, I suppose ?" I say, a painful conviction that Lenore is speaking truth forcing itself on my mind. "Now that I think of it, there was something familiar to me in the broad gold arrow she wore in her hair."

Silence for a few moments, while we stare at one another blankly.

"I wish they *had* gone on to 'The Krone' now," says Lenore drily.

"If we wait to go up Piz Languard till we go up with them," I say with a vexed laugh, " we shall remain some time at the foot, I think."

" *How* glad they will be to see us," cries Lenore, breaking out into violent merriment, that does not, however, express any equally violent enjoyment, " considering that last time they saw us they left us with the Elizabethan sentiment that ' God might forgive us, but they never would,' or words to that effect."

" I declare I do not know what you are laughing at," says Sylvia pettishly, with her eyes full of tears ; " it is a great thing to be easily amused ; as for me, I see nothing amusing in it ! This sort of thing never happens to anyone but me ; really *good* people, that one would have liked to know *en intimes*——" .

" Listen," I say, leaving the window and approaching the door, " they are coming up ! I hear Madame Enderlin's voice."

" We shall be always meeting them on

the stairs," says Sylvia lachrymosely, "and I declare I shall no more know how to behave—very likely they will take their cue from me—whether to stop and shake hands, or bow and pass on——"

"Stop and shake hands with the man— bow and pass on to the women," says Lenore promptly; "men are always kind."

"As for *you*," retorts Sylvia, turning upon her with a tearful spitefulness, "in your case there can be no difficulty; they will cut *you*, of course, out and out—*dead* —and really, considering all things, one cannot blame them."

"Of course they will," replies Lenore calmly, though her colour deepens; "I should think very meanly of them if they did not."

" And *you*" (speaking very rapidly, while the large tears still roll helplessly down her cheeks), " what will you do? how will you take it?"

" *Do?*" says Lenore with a little dry laugh ; " what *is* there to do ? I shall *be* cut, I suppose, and try to look as if I liked it."

CHAPTER IV.

WHAT JEMIMA SAYS.

"MADAME *est servic !*" says Menga, half an hour later, opening my door, and putting her head in.

"Do not go without me!" cries Sylvia, eagerly; "wait for me. Did you ever see anybody so silly as I ? I am trembling all over—like a leaf—feel!"

"Lenore is not quite ready," I say.

"We will go without her," rejoins Sylvia, quickly; "why should not we ? They

will be more likely to speak to us if she is
not by."

I shrug my shoulders. " I suppose one
must begin to be civilised again," continues
my sister, holding out one plump and
shapely arm for me to clasp a bracelet on.
" It is astonishing how soon one gets out
of the way of it ! Certainly it is cold ; but
bundled up in a shawl one looks as if one
had no more shape than the Tun of Hei-
delberg."

We descend. The few visitors are col-
lecting in the hard-scrubbed *salle à manger*
round the snow-white table.

" How my heart is beating !" says
Sylvia, as we stand at the door about to
enter ; " look and see whether they are
down yet."

I peep. " Yes, there they are ;" and as
ill-luck will have it, their places are next
ours ; you need not have taken off your
shawl ; they have both shawls, and the

husband—what is his name ?—I never can
recollect—Lascelles, is not it ?—is in his
greatcoat.   There is no help for it ; if we
wish for food, we must go into the lion's
jaws to get it.   As we approach it becomes
evident to us that the fact of our presence
has been previously revealed to the new-
comers.   As we reach the table they just
look up, and bow—gravely and slightly, it
is true ; but still they bow.   Old Mrs.
Scrope holds her little hooked nose—
gently, not Jewishly hooked—rather more
aloft than usual, gathers her shawl with a
chilly gesture about her, and says across
the table to her daughter :

"I wonder why they do not light the
stove ?"

Mr. Lascelles rises and shakes hands
heartily, and says :

" How are you ?   Deuced cold, is not it ?
How long have you been here ?"

Everybody but Lenore is down ; the

little *bourgeois* German family — father,
mother, two daughters, the mild and haver-
ing English old maid in noisome cameo
brooch and hair bracelet, who spends her
life in marauding about the Continent in
virgin loveliness ; the Cantab, who has been
climbing every high mountain in the neighbourhood, till all the skin is peeling off his
blistered scarlet face—here they are, all of
them, each eating soup, if you like to call it
soup, after his several manner. It is weak
and watery stuff enough, one would think,
but apparently too strong for the German
stomachs ; at least having nearly finished
their share, they call for hot water, pour
some into their plates, and begin to ladle it
up into their mouths.

" I had better go and call Lenore," I say
aloud to Sylvia, purposely speaking the
obnoxious name to see what effect it will
produce. " I cannot think what has become of her."

As I speak she enters. As she comes
hurriedly across the room with a sort of
nervous defiance in her face, I look at her
curiously, trying to see her as a stranger
would. Surely there can be nothing very
provocative of wrath — of conciliation,
rather—in her altered look. Even to *me*,
who have watched her daily, hourly, she
seems ill, shrunken, drooped. How much
more to them who have not seen her since
—six months ago—she shone upon them
in the healthy bloom of her delicate ripe
beauty. Poor soul ! now that her strength
is gone and her fairness waned, can they
be angry with her still ? As they rather
feel than see her approach, I am sensible
of a sort of ladylike stiffening and drawing-
up on the part of the two women.

Mr. Lascelles is fully occupied in making
faces at his soup. The dead cut Sylvia
predicted is imminent. As she slips into
her seat, the only one left—one next Mrs.

Lascelles—with eyes determinedly down-cast, and an uneasy red look, half challeng-ing, half deprecatory, on her face, curiosity gets the better of their dignity, and they both glance at her. I see them both start perceptibly. Yes, they have noticed it too. Alas! the change is too patent to escape the carelessest, hostilest eye. With a sudden impulse they both bow, as they had bowed to us, slightly, unsmilingly, without the smallest attempt at cordiality, but still quite politely.

" Deuced cold, is not it ?" says Mr. Las-celles, turning, with an air of the greatest friendliness to Sylvia; man-like, happily and sublimely ignoring the squabbles of his womankind ; and, rubbing his hands, "when last I saw you, it was deuced cold too ; we were as nearly as possible snowed up on our way back to London—do you remember, Blanche ?"

At this happy allusion to our last merry

meeting we all wax deeply, darkly, beautifully red.

"Is it always cold here?" asks Mrs.
Lascelles, rushing hurriedly, and quite contrary to her original intention, as I feel,
into conversation with me.

"It has been cold since we came, but we
are hardly fair judges yet ; we have only
been here a week ; I am told that it is a
remarkably healthy climate," I answer,
stiffly and tritely ; my besetting sin always
being a tendency to sink into an echo of
Murray.

"It has been *arctic !*" says Sylvia to her
neighbour, with a plaintive up-casting of
her eyes to his face, "positively *arctic !*
How I envy you your greatcoat !—nothing
so pretty as beaver" (stroking it delicately) ; " naturally, we left all our furs behind us."

"One peculiarity of the climate," say I,
addressing everybody, in a monotonous reci-

tative, "is, that meat killed in the autumn dries of itself in the course of the winter ; it is considered an excellent thing for making blood, and looks like sausage."

" Is not it too cold for *you?*" Mrs. Lascelles asks, pointedly addressing her question to Lenore, and speaking with a compassionate inflection in her voice.

Lenore blushes furiously. " For *me!*" she says, stammering, and looking surprised, " for—for all of us ; we *all* shiver."

No one makes any rejoinder.

" It is a wonderful climate for consumption, I believe," continues Lenore, speaking hurriedly and hesitatingly, as if not at all sure of the reception a speech from her may meet with. " A clergyman in the last stage came to St. Moritz last year, and is now quite recovered ; not" (looking round with a nervous laugh) " that *that* need be any great recommendation to any of us, I hope."

Again they look at her, with an unwilling
startled pity in their healthy prosperous
faces. The German father is dexterously
whisking his beef gravy into his mouth on
the blade of his knife, at the imminent risk
of slitting his countenance from ear to ear ;
the Cantab is reluctantly turning his peeled
nose and flayed cheeks to the old maid,
who, gently blinking behind her spectacles,
is addressing him.

*   *   *   *   *   *   *

" A happy deliverance," cries Sylvia,
stretching herself on the sofa in our sitting-
room, when at length we attain that haven,
dinner being ended. " Nothing *prostrates*
one so much as these little social ordeals !
Did you see how I cultivated the husband ?
I do not think they quite liked it."

I am looking out of window, and con-
templating Mr. Lascelles' back, as he
stands on the doorstep talking to Kolb,

and banging his arms together like a cab-
man to keep them warm. I can feel, by
the expression of his shoulders, that he is
for the third time remarking that " It is
deuced cold."

" If he had his own way, he would be
always with us, in and out, in and out,"
continues Sylvia ; "one can foresee that.
But no doubt he will not be *let*."

" What a thing it is to be thin !" cries
Lenore, with a rather bitter little laugh.
" If I had been fat and well-liking, they
would have cut me dead. If I gain in
favour in the same ratio in which I lose in
flesh they will soon be thoroughly fond of
me." I turn from the window with a sigh
at this speech. " There *is* something very
affecting in having a thing like a bird's
claw held out to you, is not there ?" continues she, looking with a sort of pensive
derision at her own hand, first opening it

and then clenching it, to see how strongly the knuckles and bones start out.

" Do not !" I say, crossly.   " I wish you would not !"

" In books," continues she, " whenever people on their death-beds lift up their thin hands, or hold out their thin hands, one always begins to cry, don't you know ?"   I laugh, but not very jocundly.   " If they could hear the way in which I cough at night I am not sure that they would not kiss me," says the young girl, with a sarcastic smile.

" How extraordinarily like Charlie his sister is !" says Sylvia, sitting up on the sofa.   " What are you looking at, Jemima ? Any new arrivals ?   Thoroughly *bon genre* they all look.   Say what you will, blood must show."

" As the old maid said when her nose got red," retorts Lenore.

" A plain likeness, of course," pursues

Sylvia, not deigning to heed this profane illustration. "Blanche Lascelles is too much of a *peace-and-plenty-looking* woman to please me—too *redundant*, don't you know? I confess to liking to see people keep within bounds : but she is growing so enormously large, she will soon be all over everywhere."

"Perhaps it is *bon genre* to spread," says Lenore mockingly ; "who knows ?"

"She put me so much in mind of him that it was on the tip of my tongue to ask after him," continues Mrs. Prodgers.

"I am very glad it remained on the tip."

"I wish with all my heart he was here," says Sylvia, continuing her monologue and yawning. "I wonder is there any chance of it ? One abuses them when one has them, but certainly life—travelling life especially—is very *triste* without a man."

"Do you wish it too, Lenore ?" I ask, walking over to where my youngest sister

is listlessly lying back in the one-arm chair
that the room affords.

" How do I know ?" she answers in
a tone of weary irritability. " I wish a
hundred things one half of the day which I
unwish the other half. No, certainly I do
not—not until I get my looks up again.
Jemima" (gazing wistfully up at me), "how
long do you think it will be before I do ?"

" My dear, am I a prophet ?" I say, very
sadly, stroking her hair.

" Evidently they thought me very much
gone off, did not they ?" she asks, with her
eyes still fixed on my face, and a faint, a
very faint hope of contradiction in her own.

" How do I know ?" I reply, evasively.
" If they *had* thought so they would hardly
have chosen *me* to confide it to."

" But they did," returns she gently,
shaking her head. " As Sylvia says, one
has one's instincts." (A moment's silence.)
" Who was it ?" she continues, with a

melancholy smile; "Madame du Barri, was not it, who said that she would rather be dead than ugly? Pah!" (with a shudder), "it would be very disagreeable to be either."

CHAPTER V.

"The gods may release
That they made fast;
Thy soul shall have ease
In thy limbs at the last;
But what shall they give thee for life, sweet life, that
is overpast?"

WHAT JEMIMA SAYS.

AT least it is summer to-day; the sun says, "Now it is *my* turn!" With his strong right hand, he has swept the clouds away from the snow-peaks—away—away—anywhere; he will have none of them. Those snow-peaks! They dazzle one so that one cannot look at them, save through blue spectacles. It makes one's eyes drop water but to glance hastily at their shining magnificence. Oh happy consummation! it is too hot even for *demi-saison* dresses.

"I think Kolb is very tyrannical!" says Sylvia, discontentedly. "What do I care about the waterfall, or the Mortiratsch glacier? After all, when you have seen one glacier you have seen them all; and though nobody *can* be fonder of scenery than I am, yet of course there are other things in the world; I had much rather have stayed at home to-day and found out what the Scropes' plans were."

We are all joggling along in a little chaise, drawn by a fat pony, which however is so far from us as to be almost out of sight, from the length of the traces—jiggling joggling along through Pontresina, between the green-shuttered white houses; here and there a flourish of flowers—gera-

niums, cinerarias—out of their windows;
through the upper village, and along the
hot high road. On each side of us is the
lovely riot of the meadow flowers; they
seem to have rushed out, all at once, and
all together, to answer to their names at
the roll-call of the spring sun.

" At all events," say I, laughing, " Mr.
Lascelles cannot say that it is ' deuced cold'
to-day. Pah ! how apoplectic it makes
one's head ! Oh for a good honest British
cabbage-leaf to put in one's hat !"

" There is one comfort," says Sylvia,
pursuing her own thoughts, " and that is
that there is no one they *can* become *liés*
with, in our absence, and I should think
that they were sociable sensible sort of
people, who cordially hated their own
society."

" Worse even than ours ?" asks Lenore,
with a cynical smile, from beneath the dusty
little hood, under which she is leaning back.

We leave the high road ; we turn into a byway that leads to the glacier, leads through a company of larches. They have grown up, here and there among the great strewn stones, of every shape and size— lichen-grown, green, forbidding. By-and-by we have to say good-bye to our carriage ; it can go no further ; the road breaks off.

" This is quite the most *triste* festivity I ever assisted at," Sylvia says, plaintively, as we dawdle and loiter hotly along.

" Bah ! how the midges bite ! As a rule, no one is more independent of men's society than I am, but in a case of this kind a man is indispensable to give a sort of impetus, a fillip, to the whole thing."

" Let us have luncheon," say I, with my usual material view of things ; " eating always raises one's spirits, and we can eat as well as if a regiment were looking on."

So we lunch on the short sward. The smooth smoke-coloured cattle are ringing their bells vigorously, as they browse near us, though what they eat the Lord only knows, unless they have a taste for yellow potentillas, sweet-scented daphne, and dry white bents. Kolb has stretched a mackintosh for us to sit on, and brought spiced beef that looks weirdly nasty, in sunwarmed slices, out of a marmot-skin bag ; rolls, hard-boiled eggs. A bottle of Château Margot stands under a great rock, knee-deep in yellow violets. The glacier river, the Bernina, runs madly past us, hoarsely raving to its wide stone bed, in a torrent of dirty yellow-green-white. There we lie, couched comfortably as ruminating cattle, while at our elbows and feet the gentians open their blue eyes, bluer than any woman's, deeper than any sapphire.

" How pretty they would be in artificial !" Sylvia says, pensively plucking one. " A spray for the side of the head, you know, and another for the corsage ; I am

afraid we are too far off for it to carry well,
or I would send one to Foster's in a tin-
box ; he will always copy any flower you
send him, exactly."

" Perish the thought !" says Lenore, with
a sort of lazy indignation, laying her head
down among a crowded little family of the
yellow violets, under a great split rock.

" Dark blue is not a good night-colour,
however," says Sylvia, still pursuing her
own train of meditation.

" How drowsy the river's roar makes
one !" I say, yawning, and burying my hot
face in my out-stretched arms ; " if you two
will not speak I shall be asleep in three
minutes."

" How *hideous* it is !" says Sylvia, dropping her gentian, and gazing with a sort of
disgust at the tearing flood.   " Glacier
rivers always are.   Did you ever see any
thing so dirty in your life ?   It looks as if
hundreds and thousands of washerwomen

had been washing in it with myriads of cakes of soap."

After all we never reached the glacier. If luncheon has cheered it has also ener-vated us. We content ourselves with lan-guidly strolling to the waterfall. Now we have reached it! now exertion is at an end; now we lie, lazy as lotus-eaters, on the dry warm herbage—scant, yet so sweet!—and gaze and listen, gaze and listen, for God knows how long, to the loud white beauty of the fall. Down it comes from the top of the low hill in one long snowy plunge; then a smooth sliding over the polished backs of the great stones; a curling of creamy wavelets; then another foamy leap in lightning and froth; then a green pool, where the sun is holding dazzling mirrors, too bright to look at, to the pines' dark faces. The long roar rings loud yet gentle in our ears, bringing to us a drowsy joy. Even Sylvia's grumblings are stilled—at

least we no longer hear them, Lenore and
I. We have climbed slowly and inter-
mittently up the rocks to a little plateau,
whence we can see the water's chiefest
plunge. Who can stop it? . The air is full
of its cold white powder ; a great stone
opposite is for ever wet with the cool damp
dust drifted against its shining sides.
Little lilac primulas confidently grow and
bloom in its clefts. Oh torrents and hills
and flowers, you make me drunk with
beauty ! What can be nobler than to
watch the play of God's imagination in
these silent places ?

With elbows deep sunk in gentians, and
head on hand, we lie and lie, till the sun is
marching in all his afternoon heat and
mellow glory through the pale turquoise
sky. The pines above our heads smell
divinely. There is no flower, however
sweet, that has a better fragrance than that
which the grave flowerless firs give out at

the bidding of their master, the high June
sun.   For half-hours, hours—we know not
which—neither of us have spoken.   My
eyes have long been fixed on the little
rainbow that the waterfall has caught and
held fast, with its faint green and yellow
and red, in her shining toils.   Presently,
and little by little, I cease to see the tender
colours of the prism—I cease to hear the
water's plunge and the pines' low sigh ; I
am asleep.   Whether my doze is long or
short, I do not know.   I imagine, however,
that it is not very long ; but it is broken
at last by a sharp exclamation from
Lenore.

" What are you making such a noise
about ?" I cry, starting up and rubbing my
eyes.   " One may as well be killed as
frightened to death——*Charlie ! ! !*"

Am I dreaming still ?   No ; the waterfall's voice has come back to my ears, and
the pines' woody fragrance to my nostrils.

Providence has granted Sylvia's prayer—
for a prayer it was; at least, it fulfilled the
hymn's definition of prayer :

> " Prayer is the heart's sincere desire,
>   Uttered or unexpressed."

There he stands, three paces from me,
among the juniper bushes, solid and real,
in the loose and untinted clothes that summer Britons love—stands there in all the
stalwart deep-coloured beauty of his manhood. Providence has sent us a man "to
give the whole thing a fillip." Lenore has
risen to her feet and is facing him. Their
hands are not touching, neither are they
speaking, only they are looking at one
another long and dumbly. Embarrass-
ment at the recollected hostility of their
last parting is tying Lenore's tongue as I
feel; but what is it that is giving that
look of silent painful wonder to Scrope's
face ?

" Why are you looking so hard at me ?"
she says at last, in a low voice, with a
tremulous asperity.   " Is there anything
odd about me ?   Do not you know that it
is not good manners to look so hard at
any one ?"

" I—I—beg your pardon," he says, stammering.   " I—I—did not mean—you see,
it is so long since I have seen——"

I have scrambled to my feet and shaken
the illicit noonday sleep from my eyes.
" Charlie !" I cry a second time, coming
forward ; and not being a person with any
great command of language, I add nothing
to the pertinent brevity of this observa-
tion.

He turns, and takes my ready hand in
the cool, familiar, brotherly clasp with
which, in their day, so many good and
handsome men have honoured me, and for
which I have never felt the least grateful
to them.   " Did not you know I was

coming?" he asks; "did not they tell you?"

"Not they!" reply I, laughing. "To let you into a secret, we are not quite on *confidential* terms—rather *en délicatesse*, as you may say. I dare say they thought we were not good enough to be told such a piece of news—that it would exhilarate us too much."

"They were nearly right there, I think," says Sylvia, to whom, being a little lower down, the answer to her prayer has been first vouchsafed. "It is never my way, as a rule, to make people conceited—men especially; I am sure they are bad enough, without one's helping them; but certainly, if one wishes to know how thoroughly to appreciate a friend one must come to the Engadin."

"You are glad to see me, then?" he says, stretching out his hand to her too, with a broad eager smile. The question

seems addressed to Sylvia, but his eyes
seek Lenore. " Truly, honestly, without
figure of speech ? You know I had my
doubts."

" A perfectly unjustifiable question,"
returns Sylvia, giving her head a little
playful jerk. " We totally decline to answer it, do not we, Jemima ?"

" And *you* ?" he says, impulsively, stooping over Lenore and lowering his voice a
little.

She has sat down again, and, leaning on
her elbow, is listlessly picking a bit of
daphne to pieces : the little treacherous
colour that his first sudden coming had
sent into her cheeks ebbing quickly out of
them again.

" *I !*" (with a little start). " Oh, of
course—yes, I think so—I suppose so—
why should not I be ?"

Her eyes are lifted to his ; they mean to
be kindly, but they have of late got a settled

look of weary *nonchalance*, that they could not, if they would, put away.

"What have you been doing to her?" he says, leading me a little away from the others, on pretence of looking over the slender plank bridge that crosses the fall, grasping my arm, and staring with an angry painful vehemence into my face. "They told me she was so altered that I should not know her again—*not know her again!*" —(with an accent of scorn)—"she would have to be altered indeed before *that* could come to pass. I thought they only said it to set me against her; that was why I followed you. I could not wait. My God! she *is* changed" (loosing my arm, and clenching his own hands together). "I could not have believed that any one, any young strong person, *could* be so changed in five months."

I do not answer, for the excellent reason that I cannot. My throat is choked, and

my silent tears drop on the bridge rail and
into the emerald pool beneath. One must
love something. I have not had many
people to love in my time ; nobody very
good, or that loved me much ; and for want
of them I love Lenore. I suppose he
thinks that my speechlessness comes from
callous indifference.

"You have taken no care of her," he
continues, harshly ; "you have not looked
after her. When did she ever look after
herself ? You—who are so much older
than she that one would have thought that
you would have been like a mother to
her."

He stops abruptly. She of whom we
speak has risen and followed us.

"You are talking about me," she says,
slightly smiling. "Yes ; you both look
guilty ! what are you saying ? No, I do
not care to hear ; nothing very interesting,
I dare say."

So saying, she saunters slowly away again.

"You are no wiser than you were; I see that," I remark, dashing away my tears, and trying to smile when we are again alone.

" You are mistaken," he answers, with eager quickness; " I am perfectly cured —perfectly ; and when one is once thoroughly cured of a complaint of this sort, one does not sicken again. If I had not been sure of that I would not have come near you : I would have put the width of all Europe between us."

I shake my head in a silent scepticism.

" See," he cries, earnestly, " do you remember how I used to tremble all over if my hand touched hers ?—how I grew redder than any lobster if she spoke to me ? Do I tremble now ?" (stretching out his right hand to me)—"am I red ?"

Still I am silent.

" Do you hear ?" he asks, impatiently.

" Yes," I answer, drily.   " I hear."

CHAPTER VI.

"I feel the daisies growing over me."

WHAT THE AUTHOR SAYS.

THEY are sitting, they two, the lover and the loved one, in the tiny graveyard of the little church upon the hill. They have risen up hastily from the noisy supper, where the fusty German mother had shut the window, where the fusty German daughters had made weak and steaming negus of their *vin ordinaire*, on this sultry summer evening. They two, and Jemima. They have passed through the small still

street, along the silent road, where even
the dust lies quiet and white, and does not
harry one as in the day time; up the lane,
past cottages and fields, to the little church
that stands below the rocky mountain.
Lenore has ridden; she could not have
walked so far up the hill-side; ridden the
fat pony, "a beautiful pony, just like a teapot," as Kolb, with doubtful compliment,
remarked of him. Now he is tied to the
church porch and is eating forget-me-nots
in the evening grey. Jemima has discreetly
strolled away, but her discretion has pleased
but one of her companions; the other has
hardly noticed it. It is all one to Lenore
whether she goes or stays. It is eight
o'clock. Pontresina church is telling the
hour sonorously, and the little hill church
beside her is answering with its one grave
bell; the church, with its rude stone tower
and little extinguisher top, its windows
deep set in the wall, like deep-sunk eyes.

" Lenore," says Scrope, presently pluck-
ing a great forget-me-not, twice the size of
those we see in England, from one of the
low graves, " do you think it wicked to tell
lies ?"

" It depends," she answers, laughing
slightly. " I think truth is rather an over-
rated virtue."

" I told a gigantic lie yesterday."

" Did you ?" she answers, but she does
not seem to care to ask what it is.

He waits a moment, but finding that her
curiosity will not come to his aid, volun-
teers his information.

" I—I—told Jemima that I was perfectly cured," (reddening a little).

" Yes, that was not quite true," she replies, quietly.

" Are you glad or sorry ?" he asks,
eagerly.

She has plucked two blades of fine grass,
and is carefully measuring them, to see

which is the taller. Perhaps that is the
reason that her response comes slowly.

"I am glad," she says, "quite glad!
Formerly, when I was strong and well, I
did not mind who cared for me or who did
not; I cared for myself a great deal—
immensely—and that was enough; but now
that I am so weak and sickly, and *wang-
ling*, as they say in Staffordshire—is not it
a good word?—does not it give a limp,
peevish, unstrung idea?—why, now I like
some good patient person to be near me,
and look sorry when I am out of breath
and in tiresome pain."

He does not answer, but I do not think
she takes his silence ill.

"Care for me," she says, simply, stretching out her hand, with a sort of naïveté, to
him, "care for me a little—care for me a
good deal, but do not care for me too
much; it is silly to care too much for anything; one misses it so if it goes."

He takes the hand she so frankly gives, but he is afraid violently to press or kiss it, lest, with a sudden change of mood, she may snatch it angrily away.

" Do you remember the day we parted ?" he asks, in a hesitating voice.

" Yes," she says, with a rather embarrassed laugh, " to be sure I remember. We both went into heroics, and you, after abusing me in good nervous English, fell on your knees before me, and in so doing gave pug's nose such a kick that it has never been the same feature since."

" It is nearly six months since then," he says, in a low voice ; " five at least. If I had taken you at your word——"

" I am so glad you did not," she interrupts, hastily.

His face falls.

" So glad, are you ?   Why ?"

" Do not you know that I like to take all and give nothing ?" she says, with a sort of smile. " That was always my way—always; let me have it a little longer. I know that I cause you pain every time that I am with you, but somehow I do not mind—I have no remorse ; you are strong, and pain does not kill ; sometimes it braces. See, I have suffered a good deal, and I am not dead."

He clasps the slight cool hand he holds tighter.

" Thank God, no !"

" Have you ever known what it is to be very unhappy ?" she says, looking with a sort of pensive curiosity into his face. " If I asked you you would say yes, you would swear it ; but somehow I doubt it. How clear and blue your eyes are ! They look as if they had always slept all night and smiled all day. You are not *fat*, certainly—far from it—I hate a fat man ; but how well and strongly your bones are covered !"

He does not asseverate; he makes no apology for his healthy manhood; but, I think, when he next looks in her face she knows that one may wear a sore heart and yet eat well, and have broad shoulders and a stalwart presence. There is no sound but the wind speaking pensively to the pines; the wind that makes all the meadows one cool shiver.

"Why are you so faithful?" she says, presently, with a sort of impatience in her voice. "There is no sense in it; there is something stupid in such fidelity; it is like a dog; it is not like a man, at least not like the men I have known."

A hot flush rises to the young man's face. "It *is* stupid," he says, humbly. "I have often thought so."

"Why cannot you take a fancy to some one else?" she continues, sharply; "to one of my sisters, for instance; not Sylvia —no, I do not think I can conscientiously recommend her—but Jemima; she would worship the ground you trod on; and she is not so *very* old, either. I have heard some people say that an Englishwoman is at her prime, mind and body, at twenty-eight, and she is only twenty-nine."

Scrope does not seem to jump at the tempting offer thus made him; he looks down on the flowery grass at his feet.

"She is not much to look at, certainly," pursues Lenore, coolly, "but neither am I, for that matter, just now; but of course, when I grow strong again I shall get my looks back, shall I not?"

He is busy, apparently, in trying to make out the Romansch inscription on the small broken pillar beside him; at least he does not reply.

"Why do not you answer me?" she cries, angrily. "You used to be glib enough with your compliments and fine speeches ; if you cannot say 'Yes,' at least have the honesty to say 'No.'"

"My dear," he says, with a sort of tremor in his voice, "what should I say either 'Yes' or 'No' to ? In my eyes you have never lost your looks ; how can you get back what you have not lost ?"

She looks at him with a scared discontent in her pale face. "You have got out of it very lamely," she says, with a brusque laugh. "I never heard anything clumsier in my life. There—never mind. I suppose you could not help it."

Her eyes stray thoughtfully away to the hills ; a luminous mist, a dimness, yet a glory—seems spread over the high mountain amphitheatre that looks down on Pontresina ; great glorious battlements, lifting high heads against the higher heaven — citadels that a God must be dwelling in : that dim effulgence is the skirt of his trailed robes. Below, the meadows flash in yellow, and the river twists in silver. Oh, heavenly Zion! oh, fair City beyond the clouds! can thy jasper walls and pearly gates be yet fairer?

" And you find that it is quite as impossible as you did six months ago?" Scrope asks, with a tremble in his low voice, after they have sat silent some time.

" Quite," she answers, briefly.

" And it is always *he* that is in the way?" he says, with an accent of bitterness.

" Yes," she answers, softly; "always he —always he." (Then with a dreamy smile) " You see that there are other people who can be stupidly, *doggishly* faithful, as well as you; *you*, at least, cannot blame me."

" If he did but know it!" the young man cries, smiting his hands together, and looking passionately upwards to the faint skies above him; "if some one would but tell him—if he did but see you now—he could not keep his senseless resentment any longer. It is against my own interest to say so, but he could not, he *could* not."

"He has no resentment against me now," she answers, quickly, "none; he is no longer angry with me."

"How do you know?" with a hasty suspicion in his voice; "has he written to you?"

" No."

" How then?"

" I have seen him," she says, briefly.

For a moment, astonished disappointment keeps him silent; then the two words, "When, where?" come low, but hurriedly, from his mouth.

"We had a long talk," she says, with the same unmirthful, tender smile, "quite a long talk—on a bridge—in the moonlight, at Bergun ; the accessories sound romantic, do not they ? Moonlight always makes one feel sentimental ; I am not quite sure that we were not a little so."

A pause. Through the larches in the wood above them, a long, long sigh passes ; then falls—dies—then revives again ; a sound as of infinite yearning.

" When he is coming here give me warning beforehand," says Scrope, in a voice that is next door to a whisper. " I suppose he will be coming here soon ?"

" Perhaps," she answers, with a little laugh that is almost malicious. "Who knows ? Perhaps he may take it in his wedding tour."

"His wedding tour ! !"

" Yes," she answers, looking away from his bewildered face again, on the perfect content, the evening placidness, of the landscape ; " it is *contrariant*, is it not ? but he is going to be married."

" Who told you so ?" (very rapidly).

" He told me so himself."

" And *you ?* how did you take it ? what did you say ?"

" I said, 'Oh, are you ?' I believe I laughed—I am not sure."

" And then ?"

" And then—no, not quite *then* " (drawing in her breath slowly)—" a little afterwards—he went."

" And you ?"

" And I—oh, I lay down on the grass—nice crisp dry grass, by the river, with my head in a clump of trefoil—what a noisy river it was !" (speaking with a sort of pensive complaint)—" sometimes I hear it now, at night, running through my head."

" And you stayed there all night—*you*—in the damp ?" (with a tone of reproachful solicitude).

" No, not *all* night ; about half the night,

I think—I forget about the time ; talking is very tiring work, and I was tired."

" Yes ?"

" And then they grew anxious—Jemima and Sylvia—and came to look for me."

" Well ?"

" And then they scolded me, and asked me what had happened to me, and I said I had seen a ghost ; so I had."

The wind has no more to say ; he has dropped ; there is no noise but the swirl of the far water.

" Sylvia was quite interested," pursues Lenore, rousing herself, and even looking rather amused ; " she wanted to know what sort of a ghost it was—whether a man's or a woman's, or a child's or a dog's—she said she had heard of dog's ghosts being some-times seen—and also whether it carried its head under its arm ? I said, ' No it did not' and—and—and—that is all, I think."

On the glacier mountain there is a white

glory, that cannot be moonlight, for moon is there none ; it must have stolen some of the sunset, and kept it in its bosom ; the shadows steal over the lower snow, but the peaks keep that strange shining, such as Moses' face had when he came down from his high talk with God.

"Charlie," says Lenore, suddenly, with an abrupt change of subject, "does not it occur to you that at Pontresina the dead are much better lodged than the living ? Would not you rather be here than at the *Croix Blanche ?*"

"At the present moment, certainly," he answers, with a smile. "I prefer *you* and the smell of flowers to the German squaws and the smell of negus."

"Look," she says, rising from her grassy seat, " I am going to show you something. If I were old, or had any complaint that was likely to kill me, I will show you the exact spot where I should like to lie—how

can you see? you have turned away your
face—pshaw! how absurdly sensitive you
are; you are as bad as Jemima. If either
of _you_ were to point out to me the place
that you wished to be your grave I should
listen with the most composed attention,
and try to bear it in mind against the time
when I should have the misfortune to lose
you."

"I quite believe it," he answers bitterly;
"I have no doubt you would."

"See," she says, not heeding the bitterness, hardly hearing it, but pointing, with a
smile, to a spot of ground, richer even than
its neighbours in manifold-coloured flowers
and fine green grass, "did you ever see
anything so luxurious? This wall's shadow
to shelter one from the sun at noonday,
and all these pink plantains to ripple above
one's head; they say one does not hear
when one is dead—well, as to that, I have
my own opinion; but if one _could_ hear, it

would be pleasant to listen to the wind
softly buffetting their tall heads in the dim
summer nights, would not it ?"

No answer.

" I would have no gilt tears, however, on
my cross," she adds, a few minutes later.

He stoops and plucks a handful of the
pink plantains angrily, and then throws it
away again.

" What are you doing ?" she asks, turning with a gesture of surprise and remonstrance to him ; " why do you look so
cross ? Why are you frowning and clenching your hands ? You foolish fellow, do
you think if I meant to die *really* that I
should talk about it so lightly—that I
should pick and choose my grave ? Good
God! no !" (with a strong shudder)—" I
should keep far enough from the subject !"

CHAPTER VII.

"On pain of death, let no man name death to me; it is a word infinitely terrible."

WHAT THE AUTHOR SAYS.

"YES, they are certainly coming round," says Sylvia, with a tone of self-gratulation. "I met Mrs. Scrope just now on the stairs, and she said, 'You have been to the Rosegg? I hear there is quite a practicable road there.' When once one has the *men* on one's side one is all right; and somehow we always manage to enlist the sympathies of the fathers and husbands and brothers."

" I do not agree with you," says Jemima, taking her hat off and laying it on the table. " I think it is just the other way— the *women* to be propitiated, and the *men* follow naturally. Take care of the women and the men will take care of themselves."

" They certainly dress very well," continues Sylvia complacently; " nothing *voyant;* all those pretty mouse-colours, and sad colours, and smoke colours, that I am so devoted to. Very good taste ; and say what you will, *that* alone is enough to prepossess one in people's favour."

*   *   *   *   *   *   *

" I have just been falling into the arms of that dreadful little widow," Mrs. Scrope says, re-entering her own apartment at the same time as Sylvia has made her re-appearance in hers. " Ambling up the stairs and coquetting with the banisters, as usual. She is *always* on the stairs."

" She reminds me of the women in Isaiah, don't you know ?" says Mrs. Lascelles, laughing ; " ' walking and mincing as they go.' I wonder had they high-heeled shoes and a panier ? If it were the fashion to sew pillows to armholes nowadays, what gigantic *bolsters* she would have !"

" My dear, atrociously as that girl behaved, we never can be too thankful to her for having delivered us from the Prodgers connection. *Prodgers !*—such a name !"

" Do not holloa before you are out of the wood," says Mr. Lascelles, looking up from his novel for a moment, and instantly immersing himself in it again.

" I believe what first set her against him was the awful description I gave her of *our* honeymoon," says his wife, laughing again. " I told her about your being sea-sick all the way to St. Malo. I remember she looked awe-struck at the time."

" It will be all on again before you can look round," says Mr. Lascelles, again emerging from his romance.

Both women shake their heads.

·" Poor soul ! it would hardly be worth while her being ' on,' as you say, with any one."

" You mean that she is not long for this world ?" replies he, dropping his book entirely this time. Mr. Lascelles' voice is never as low as Cordelia's, and the door is ajar.

" Hush !" cry both the women together. " Some one is passing ; it may be one of them."

" I wish I could induce you *sometimes* not to speak at the very tip-top of your voice," says his wife. " If you remember, when you proposed to me, at the Inniskillings' ball, you expressed your wishes so loudly that you drowned the band."

WHAT JEMIMA SAYS.

THE hotel is fuller than it was. This last
week has made a difference. Several more
little whitewashed rooms are occupied. A
member of the Alpine Club, with a harem
of three gaunt women, battered and un-
sexed by much scaling of high mountains;
two or three new couples. The last, an
elderly clergyman and his wife, occupy the
room next mine. Only this morning I was
remarking on the thinness of the partition
walls: I can hear him alternately splashing
and groaning in his tub.

"They have not been married long,"
Lenore says. "They say the Lord's
Prayer together very loudly every night."

And Scrope asks, laughing, whether that
is a proof of being newly wedded.

This was after breakfast. Since then
we have been to the Rosegg glacier. Lenore has not been with us: gradually she

is slipping out of our excursions. " For
the present," she says ; "just for the present, I am better at home." Now we are
back again, Sylvia and I, in our own little
sitting-room—a cheerful little place, whence
one can look down on the white houses of
the clean narrow street, see the out-goers
and incomers to the hotel, and catch bright
glimpses of the mountains.

The door opens and Lenore enters, and
at the same moment Sylvia passes out.
" Is she gone ?" says Lenore, advancing
towards me ; "*really* gone, do you think ?
I do not know why I ask ; I have nothing
particular to say." Her face is disturbed,
and her eyes wander uneasily round. " I
—I—I have been *eavesdropping*," she says,
beginning to laugh. " What do you think
of that ? And they say listeners never
hear any good of themselves. That, however, is not a case in point, for I heard
nothing about myself, of course—*nothing.*"

" Eavesdropping !" I repeat, surprised.
" That is not very like you.   What do you
mean ?   What are you talking about ?"

" I was passing by the Scropes' door just
now," she says, with a sort of hurry and
agitation in her manner—" it was ajar, I
wish people would keep their doors shut,"
(with a tone of irritability)—" and they
were talking ; the man—the husband—you
know what a sweet low voice he has—was
saying in a tone as loud as all the bulls you
ever heard bellowing : ' She is not long for
this world.'   Whom do you think they
were talking about ?"

" My dear child," I say impatiently,
" what extraordinary things excite your
curiosity !   Am I a diviner of dark say-
ings ?   Probably some friend of their own
that we never heard of."

" And then the woman said, ' Hush,
hush !' " pursues she, with her eyes still
watching my face.   " Why did they say

' Hush ?' if it were some friend of theirs, why should they mind being overheard ? They were saying no ill of her."

" Pshaw !" say I, pettishly ; " how do I know !"

" He said *she*, certainly—not *he*," she continues, as if unable to leave the sub-ject. " *Not long for this world ?*" (uttering the words very slowly). " Poor soul, whoever she is I am very sorry for her, are not you, Jemima ?"

" Yes, yes, of course—very sorry," I answer, indistinctly, turning to the window.

" And yet it is absurd to be sorry for a person one has never seen—never heard of —is not it ?" persists Lenore, again breaking out into a laugh. " Perhaps we are throwing away our compassion—perhaps it was a dog or a cat—who knows ?"

" Very likely, very likely !"

" But why did they say ' Hush ?' " she says, brooding over the word, and addressing the question rather to herself than to me.

I do not answer.

" Jemima," she says, following me to the window, " look round—I hate not being listened to when I am talking—I am going to make you laugh—you often laugh at my ideas; well, they are sufficiently ridiculous now and then ; do you know I took it into my head—one is so egotistical—that per- haps they were talking of—of—me."

I lean out of the window, and try to persuade myself that my voice, as I say " *Nonsense*," sounds lazily indifferent.

" You are not laughing," she cries, in a tone of alarm. " I thought you would have laughed. Why do not you laugh ? Is it possible that you see nothing ridicu- lous in it—that you think it—it—is— *true ?*"

" I think nothing of the kind," I answer irritably ; " do not be so absurdly fanciful."

"If they *did* mean me," she says, with the same restless strained laugh, "they are alone in their opinion, are not they?—*quite* alone. It does *me* no harm, and it amuses them, I suppose—ha, ha!"

"What disease do they mean to kill me by, I wonder?" she says after a pause, spent by her in rapidly traversing and re-traversing the little room. "Consumption, of course" (shuddering) . . . . "They should have seen you last winter," she re-sumes by-and-by, standing beside me, and uneasily trying to see my face, "when you had that attack of influenza. How you coughed! Worse, far worse, than I do, and your head ached torturingly—mine seldom aches—and you were so weak you could scarcely lift a finger, and yet it was only influenza!"

"Only influenza," I echo mechanically; "influenza is nothing."

"Tell me," she says, a little reassured,

and looking into my face as if she would *wring* from me the answer she longs for, " you must have an opinion one way or the other ; do you *think* they meant me ?"

" My dear," I say, driven into a corner, " did I hear what they said ? I only know what you tell me—it—it—is very conceited of you to imagine that they must be always talking of you."

" People are so fond of killing their friends, are not they ?" she says, with the same wistful searching look in her great and lovely eyes ; "so are doctors, and very often the killed outlive the killers after all."

" Very often."

" Next time that I pass their door I shall run past with my fingers in my ears. Feel how my heart is beating !"

" You are growing as bad as Sylvia," I say, trying to speak gaily ; she is always requesting me to feel how her heart is beating; if you *both* set up nerves I shall decamp."

" You think I may make my mind quite easy," she says, in a lighter tone, taking my hand in her two hot slender ones.

" Of course, of course."

" That they were talking of some one else—or that if it *were* me, they were utterly and unaccountably mistaken ?"

" To be sure! to be sure!"

"Fat and florid people often seem to think that those who are not red and bulky as themselves must be in *articulo mortis.*"

" So they do."

" Jemima!" (still strongly clasping my hand in both hers), " if you believe it so firmly, you will not mind *swearing* it."

" What is the use of oaths and asseverations ?" I ask, uncomfortably. " Will not a simple assertion do as well ?"

"You *won't* swear!" she cries, in a tone of profound alarm. " Why not ? Jemima,

I do not like your face! Your eyes will not meet mine—your lips are quivering— you are half crying. I know that I am very sick—that I have not much peace, day or night—but you do not think that it means anything bad ?—that I am—oh, my God! I cannot say the word !"

Her sentence breaks off, smothered in a shuddering sob.

"I think nothing of the kind," I say, hastily, thoroughly frightened at her agita- tion "Why *will* you gallop away with an idea ? Oh, Charlie ! *do* come here ; she is *so* impracticable—*so* unreasonable—she is talking *such* nonsense."

The door has opened, and Mr. Scrope is looking doubtfully in. At my words he enters hastily.

For the first time in her life she runs to him of her own accord, and throws herself into his arms. " Oh, Charlie !" she cries, wildly, "you are the only person in the

world that is kind to me. They have been
so cruel to me—so cruel. They have been
saying such things of me—you would not
believe it. That man—that Mr. Lascelles
—says I am not long for this world, and
Jemima quite agrees with him."

"Jemima is a fool!" says Mr. Scrope
unjustly, looking with a momentary expression of raging hatred at me over her prone
head.

"*Not long for this world!*" she repeats,
with a sort of moan, lifting her face, and
staring pitifully into his. "Those were his
very words : I have not altered one."

"Lout! idiot!" cries Scrope, angrily ;
"he had not an idea what he was saying !
—he never has. My darling" (closely
straining her to his heart, as if neither
God, nor his great angel, Death, should
avail to tear her thence), "please God, you
are longer for this world than he is—than
I—or Jemima—or any of us."

"Do you mean it, *really ?*" she says, with an awful anxiety in her tone. "Are you serious ? Oh, God ! how I wish I could think so."

"Are you so anxious to outlive us all ?" he asks, with a passionate melancholy. "Well, I daresay—it is natural, I suppose. Why should not you ? Very likely you will have your wish."

"I want to live to be *quite* old," she says, hurriedly, not heeding his upbraiding eyes or tone. "I want to live a great many years : people are often happier when they are middle-aged than in youth ; but it is pleasant to be young, too. It is not *all* pleasure, but there is a great deal. I do not complain—I do not complain." (She is trembling violently.) "Hold me !" she says, hysterically. "Do not let me go. You are the only person in the world to whom it matters much whether I die or live. Promise me that I shall not—oh! that dreadful word!—promise me!"

" I promise, darling," he says, " I promise."

" You speak uncertainly!" she says, wrenching herself out of his arms, and staring at him in a distrustful agony; " you are like Jemima—your face is all quivering. I believe you are telling me falsehoods on such a subject! Great God! can there be anything wickeder than to deceive one—to tell one lies—in such a case ?"

" Oh, my dear, I am not telling lies! Before God, I am not! I confidently trust—I altogether hope, that I shall yet see you strong and well as ever again. If I thought the contrary, do you think I could bear my own life for one minute ?"

" What does it matter what you think— what you hope ?" she cries, roughly, with

one of her old petulant movements; "will
your trusting and hoping keep it off?
Will telling lies about it make it any
better?" (with an angry flash of her lovely
miserable eyes at us both). "Whatever
you say—whatever you do—it is coming!
it is coming!"

She flings herself down on the little
sofa, shuddering from head to foot, and
buries her face in the pillow, while her
whole frame is shaken by the violence of
her sobs.

"My dearest child!" I say, half out of
my sober wits with fright and pain, advancing to her, and gently touching her on the
shoulder; "for Heaven's sake do not be so
excited! You are not very ill now, really,
you know; you can go about a little, and
walk, and talk like the rest of us; but if
you behave in this way——"

"Where have my eyes been?" she interrupts, sitting up again, and speaking

connectedly, but not calmly, while the great tears pour down her cheeks; "how is it that I have not seen all your looks and signs ? If they had not thought me very bad would the Scropes have spoken to me the other night ? Not they ! So I excited their *compassion*, did I ? I had no idea that I was an object of *pity !* I never used to be. Oh, I am indeed ! They were right ! I am indeed !" (breaking into a fresh tempest of great sobs, and again hiding her face in the cushion).

"You are mistaken!" cries Scrope, beside himself at the sight of her agony, and throwing himself on his knees; " Look up, Lenore ! Look up, beloved ! Look in my face, and see whether I am telling truth ; they talked to you the other night because they knew that if they were not civil to you I should never speak to them again—because they *dared* not be impertinent to you. Why *should* they pity you, except for being younger and prettier than themselves ? "

" You may save your breath," she answers, looking at him fixedly, with a sort of resentment ; " there is no untrue thing that you would not say to me now, to keep me quiet. . . . It is very unjust," she cries out loud, clasping her lifted hands in a frenzy ; " it is hard—there is no sense in it—that I, that am the youngest, should go first ! I, that was so pretty, and enjoyed my life so much ! Some people only *half* live ; until we went to Dinan I lived every moment of my life ! Since then I have been miserable, certainly—very miserable now and then—but it was not half so bad as this ! Oh ! how gladly I would have it all over again !—at least I was *alive* then," she says, trembling violently ; " nobody pitied me *then !* After all, what does it matter what happens to one, so long as one is alive !—*that* is the great thing !

Sometimes I have said I wished I was dead ; but God knows I did not mean it—one says so many things that one does not mean—he *cannot* be so cruel as to take me at my word ! Oh, he cannot ! he cannot !"

Her voice dies in a wail—a wail of unspeakable fear.

" Good Heavens ! what is the matter ?" says Sylvia, opening the door and entering ; her commonplace voice striking on us with a painful incongruity. " Why are you all pulling such long faces ?"

We none of us answer her.

CHAPTER VIII.

"Though one were fair as roses
    His beauty clouds and closes;
And well tho' love reposes,
    In the end it is not well."

WHAT JEMIMA SAYS.

ENORE has been very ill; her very fear has accelerated what she feared. During the night following the conversation detailed in the last chapter, in a violent fit of coughing, made more violent than usual by over-powering emotion, by uncontrolled weep-ing, she has broken a blood-vessel. It is in the dead of night; every soul in the hotel is asleep. Until they have tried it, no one can realise the feeling of absolute helpless desperation that assails one under such a catastrophe happening in a remote and hardly accessible corner of Switzerland, utterly without doctors, and four days' post from England. Since the days of Lenore's childhood, I have been entirely unused to the sight of sickness. I have not the remotest idea what remedies to apply, neither is Sylvia any wiser. In my despair I turn to the one person from whom I know that I shall get at least passionate sympathy. Apparently he is not asleep, for before I knock at his door he has opened it, and stands before me in the dishevelled dress in which a person usually appears who has sprung out of sleep into their clothes, his curled locks tossed in the untidiness of slumber, and the heavy lids still weighing on his blue eyes.

" I thought it was your step," he says,

hurriedly. " God Almighty ! what is it ?
Is she—is she "——

" She is much worse ; she has broken a
blood - vessel," I answer, breathlessly.
" What are we to do ? what are we to do ?"
(wringing my hands). " No doctor to
send for ! One is so utterly helpless—
what *is* to become of us ?"

For an instant he has clenched his
hands, with a movement of despair more
absolute even than mine ; then, under the
urgent need for them, his strayed wits
come back.

" There must be a doctor at St. Moritz,"
he says, " amongst the two or three hundred visitors there always are one or two.
I will knock up M. Enderlin, and make
him saddle me a horse to go there."

" But what are we to do meanwhile ?" I
ask, helplessly. " You cannot be back for
two hours at soonest. We know nothing !
Perhaps, we may be throwing away her

life, for want of knowing the right way to
keep it."

" I will send my mother," he says.

He is already half-way down the long
chill passage. In twenty minutes more he
is gone, and the whole house is astir.
Doors are being opened ; people of both
sexes, evidently so sketchily dressed as to
avoid rather than court notice, protrude
their heads, and ask what is the matter.
Mrs. Scrope has come hurrying to us, with
the entire self-forgetfulness of a kind-
hearted person ; come hurrying in a limp
and corsetless dishabille, eminently becoming to a young girl, but cruelly trying
to the best looking woman of more ad-
vanced age. How many secrets of the
prison-house, must a fire, an alarm of
burglars, or a sudden illness, have revealed
before now. She has put something of
calm and order into our disordered con-

sternation. We do what little we can—
alas! it is but little—and then wait—wait
—try to imagine, as we sit in absolute
silence and weary stillness in the little bare
room, how far up the mountain road to St.
Moritz our messenger is; fancy a hundred
times that we hear the hoofs of his backcoming horse long before he can possibly
have reached his destination. Sylvia has
disappeared ; certainly she was here when
first I went to call Charlie, though she entirely declined to accompany me on that
mission ; has she actually had the heart to
go to bed again ? I am not long left in
doubt. As we sit, not speaking, in the
dawn of the summer morning, that seems
to have run half-way to meet the so lately
gone evening, the door opens softly and
she enters. She has been making a
toilette: an embroidered wrapper embraces
her form, and a saffron ribbon is twisted in
her black hair. The ruling passion strong

in death !—not her own death, but that of another person.

" Can I be of any use ?" she says, looking in. " Oh, Mrs. Scrope, how good of you to come to us in our trouble ! I had not an idea that you were here."

I make signs to her not to speak, and also that the room is too confined to admit of *three* nurses. She disappears. It is full morning before the joyful sound that for hours we have been straining our ears to catch greets them. The doctor has arrived. He is a dirty-looking little fellow ; some paltry apothecary probably, to whom, were one in England, one would hardly entrust the care of a sick dog ; but *now*, with what utter faith, with what intense and believing anxiety, do we listen to his *fiat !*

" He says it is only a small blood-vessel after all," I say, trying to speak cheerfully, as I rejoin Charlie outside the door, and looking haggardly into his still more haggard face, in the early splendour of the strong young daylight ; " perhaps we have been making ourselves too miserable. She is to be kept absolutely quiet; only one person at a time in the room, and that one not to speak. She is to have all sorts of nourishing things—good heavens !" (breaking off in a sort of despair) " where are they to come from—here, where there is nothing but spiced beef as hard as a shoe, and skeleton fowls ?"

" Why did you bring her here ?" he asks, in a tone of angry misery. " Were you *mad ?* It was *murder !*"

" We did it for the best," I answer, humbly ; " the doctor recommended it and she fancied it." . . . .

As ill-luck will have it, next day there is a great yearly fête celebrated in the village ; a stir and festal noise all the long day in the crowded street and through the

house ; doors banging, loud voices laughing. We have tried so earnestly to keep
them quiet, but all in vain. When one is
merry with beer, and when one has a holi-
day only twice or thrice a year, one cannot
always, every moment, bear in mind the
sufferings of an unknown unseen stranger.
It is drawing towards night again ; still
the clamour shows no symptom of abating.
Now and again I hear Madame Enderlin's
low kind voice in earnest remonstrance,
but even she remonstrates in vain. The
weather has grown very hot. Lenore lies
on her side, dozing uneasily, moaning now
and then. I sit beside her, bathing her
hot hands with eau de Cologne and water,
and give a fresh start of exasperation and
apprehension at every fresh noise that
penetrates through the door, left ajar to
admit a little air into the close room, where
open windows are forbidden, at least in the
evening. Presently, a louder noise than

any of the former ones reaches my tortured ears : a great and heavy stamping up the stairs—up—up—up. It reaches the passage on which all our doors open. I stretch my neck to see what it is, without moving, and to my horror discover that it is an Italian hurdy-gurdy man, with his instrument on his back. He is just stooping his hand to turn the handle, when I see Charlie rush wildly out of his own door and with furious gestures stop him. The poor man is much surprised. "What, must not he play for the Signora ?"

* * * * *

A month has passed. Lenore is again up ; lies on the sofa in the sitting-room, dressed ; again talks, sometimes again laughs.

"She wishes to see you," I say to Mr. Scrope, as we meet in the passage; "she is quite looking forward to it; will you go now ?" My fingers are on the door handle ; I half turn it.

"Stay," he cries, hastily, but in a low voice, putting his hand on mine to check it; "I am not ready—wait a moment—tell me—how do I look?"

"What do you mean?" I say, half-laughing; "are you taking a leaf out of Sylvia's book?"

"You know what I mean," he answers impatiently. "Do I look cheerful — in good spirits—as if I had nothing on my mind?"

I scan his face doubtfully, I cannot answer in the affirmative.

"Her eyes look me through and through," he says, excitedly, "no matter how much I lie, she is not deceived. Tell me, Mima, how can I make my face tell lies?—how can I look content?"

"She will ask you no questions," I answer, sadly; "at least, I think not—she has asked me none."

"Shall I—be—be—very much shocked?"

he asks in a whisper, " it is better to know what to expect—tell me."

" She is pulled down, of course," I answer sorrowfully ; " very much pulled down ;" (then, after a little pause) : " my poor fellow, what is the use of buoying ourselves up with untrue hopes ?   It is the beginning of the end ; the doctor himself said as much to me the other day."

CHAPTER IX.

"The light upon her yellow hair,
  But not within her eyes;
The light still there upon her hair,
  The death upon her eyes."

WHAT THE AUTHOR SAYS.

"HOW much better you are looking!"

In his own mind he has been practising this little speech—practising it with the proper intonation of half surprised cheerfulness; when he comes to pronounce it, really it is a failure. There is a strained gaiety in his tone that would hardly deceive a baby.

"More perjuries," she says, with a lan-

guid smile, looking up at him half compassionately from her couch. " I will
dispense you from telling any more stories ;
you told a great many the other day, but
I do not think they will come much against
you in the last account—but still—be on
the safe side—tell no more of them."

" I — I — I said nothing but what I
thought," he begins, with a stammering
haste, but her great clear eyes looking
steadily, though not unkindly through him,
make his voice decline into silence.

" I have done crying for myself now,"
she says, with a sort of smile, " do not you
think I have had plenty of time to do that
in, during these last long endless nights ?
I could not have believed a summer night
could be so long.   I have been sorrier for
myself than I ever was for anybody else
—but—but—I am getting used to it—I
kick and scream no longer.   Where is the
use ?".

What has become of the stiff smile into
which he has so carefully trained his features? He has taken possession of one
of her pale hands; he seems to be very
welcome to it; she does not care whether
he has it or has it not; he has stooped and
laid his bronzed cheek upon it to hide his
face.

> " ' As flies to wanton boys, so we to the gods
>   They kill us for their sport,' "

she says, dreamily repeating this couplet
out of " King Lear." " I suppose they are
killing me for their sport?"

" You are not to talk. Jemima says so,"
he says, raising his head, and speaking with
a tone of shocked distress.

" Bah!" she answers slightingly, "if I
am silent *for ever*, will it save me? Do
you think that if I thought there was the
remotest chance of *that*, I would once open
my lips? But what is the use of setting
up one's little bit of life, like an end of

candle on a save-all, to make it burn a few
moments longer ?" A little dumb pause.
" You are crying !" she says presently, with
one of her old quick and irritable moments, which contrasts oddly and painfully
with her changed and almost extinguished
voice. " I hate to see a man cry ! It is
unnatural—womanish—it always makes me
inclined to laugh."

" For God's sake, laugh, if you feel dis-
posed !" he says fiercely, dashing away his
tears, as if ashamed and angry at them.
" I have been your butt always, Lenore !
I am willing to be so still."

" Are *you* going to quarrel with me ?"
she asks, querulously. " I suppose so ;
sooner or later everybody does."

" Do they ?" (speaking softly, and again
stooping his head, to kiss her fingers).

" You blame me for talking," she says
presently, with a sort of weary pettishness,
" and then you do not volunteer a word

yourself. Some one must speak; we cannot both sit dumb—mumchance."

" You are right," he says, making a great effort to speak easily and lightly. " I am more than ordinarily stupid to-day—head-achy, I think—cobwebby."

" At' least do not look so woe-begone," she says, staring at him with discontented tired eyes; " you make it worse for me— harder. I have been trying to persuade myself that what happens to every one cannot be so very bad—but you—your face upsets me !"

" How can I mend it ?" he says, humbly and fondly. " I will try."

" After all, it is no such a great catas- trophe," she says with a little bitter laugh; " nobody is much to be pitied but me— nobody cares much except myself, and, perhaps, *you*. Jemima *thinks* she is enor- mously grieved; she pulls a long face, but it is easy to see that it will not be the

death of her—that she will survive many
long and happy years to talk about 'poor
dear Lenore.' "

He silently caresses her hand, but does
not trust himself to embark on any speech.

"How strong you are!" she says, her
eyes wandering steadily and coldly, with a
sort of envy, over his face and figure.

"Certainly there are hands and hands"
(again taking possession of her own, and
laying it beside his to compare them). "If
you do not play tricks with yourself—if
you are moderately steady—what a long
life you will probably have, full of action
and pleasure and pleasant business! Oh,
my God!"—(breaking out into the passionate and so-absolutely-useless upbraid-
ings that we sometimes address to the
great Power above us)—"it is not fair—
indeed it is not. How have you been so
much better than I, that you should live
so many happy years after I am gone?"

"Oh, my love," he cries in a tone of the acutest pain, "why do you throw my strength in my teeth? Can I help it? Do you think it gives me any pleasure? Do you think that if I could be weak and sinking like you—*now*—this minute—that I should complain much?"

"Of course you would," she answers feebly but brusquely, "as much as I do. Of course you are glad to be strong; you would be an idiot if you were not; as long as one has good health, one has *everything!* One can get over every other trouble, but that—that——".

He shakes his head dissentingly. More than once the effort of talking has brought on an access of coughing, but Scrope's remonstrances are vain; she is resolute to carry on the conversation.

"Fifty years hence you will probably still be here," she says, in the same faint envious voice. "You are twenty-eight now—yes—a hale strong man of seventy-eight—still alive—still enjoying—children and grandchildren all about you."

" Never !" he says, violently starting up, and walking about the room in disordered haste. " I shall never have a child ! If you leave me, Lenore, I shall never have a wife."

" Pooh !" she says, contemptuously, " five years hence you will be a respectable *père de famille.* What do I say ?—*Five* years ? three—two—and when you are talking about your conquests you will have to think twice before you can recollect what colour my eyes were, or which of the dry dusty hair-locks in your pocket-book was mine."

" At least you are consistent," he cries fiercely, stopping suddenly beside her, his face white and disfigured with angry grief ; " all your life your object has been to give pain. Well, I congratulate you ; weak and changed as you are in other ways, you are still unchanged in that—are still as able as ever to cut to the heart."

" Why should not I ?" she says wearily, rolling her head from side to side on the pillow. " I have been cut to the heart enough in my day ; why should not other people go shares with me ? . . . . Until we went to Dinan," she resumes by-and-by, " I had always had my own way ; I never remember the time when I had not. I always said, that if ever I did not get my own will in anything it would be the death of me. I remember telling Paul so, almost the first time I saw him ; I thought it rather a fine thing to say ; I never dreamed of it's coming true, but it has."

" Not yet—not yet !" he remonstrates, passionately.

" Not that I am dying of love," she says, raising herself and speaking with more energy than she has yet shown.

" Never say, or let any one else say, that. Whatever tales one may have heard to that effect, I do not believe any one ever did such a thing in this world. If I had not been sickly to begin with, I *could* not have fretted myself into my grave, however hard I had tried. I should have grown yellow and pinched and withered before my time, but I should have *lived*. Yes, if I had not been sickly, radically sickly, to begin with, I should have lived."

" Live now !" he cries wildly, throwing himself down on his knees beside her sofa, and looking up with all the sorrowful madness of his blue eyes into her face. " Why should not you ? Perhaps you will never again be very strong, but there is no reason why you may not live—yes, live for many years. This climate is too harsh for you ; when you grow a little stronger let me take you away to a warmer suaver one—to Italy—the South of France ; let me take

you, Lenore—take my *wife*—the only wife
I shall ever have."

"Your *wife!*" she says, with a smile
wholly sorrowful, yet touched with a little
gratification. "I thought we had heard
the last of that old story."

"*Never!*" he answers, vehemently.
"*Never!* As long as I am near you you
will *never* hear the last of it."

"If you honestly wish to marry me," she
says, looking half gratefully at him with her
large and languid eyes; "yes, you look
honest, it is a way you have; but if you
wish it seriously, it must be only as a
penance. Even good men, who have loved
their wives to begin with, if they fall sick, and
remain for a long time ailing invalids, grow
tired of them; against their will they grow
tired of them. If I lasted long enough, you
would grow tired—heartily tired—of me."

"Should I?" (with an expressive accent).
Again she shakes her head.

18—2

" There are worthier occupations in life
for a young and handsome man than carry-
ing cushions and shaking physic-bottles."

" Tastes differ," he says, smiling a little,
though not very merrily. " I think not."

" Who *could* love me now ?" she asks,
with a movement of disbelieving self-con-
tempt. " *Aimer d'amour*, I mean ; they
might love me in the sense in which good
and tender-hearted people love anything
that is miserable and suffering ; but that is
not the way in which I used to be loved—
not the way in which I care to be loved."

" Neither is it the way in which I love
you," he answers firmly.

" Why do you tantalise me ?" she cries,
angrily, pushing her heavy hair irritably
away from her blue-veined temples ; " talking about what we shall do *if I live*. I shall
not live—I shall die. Often—so often—in
the past nights, when you have all been
comfortably warmly asleep, I have said

over and over to myself, ' Lenore Herrick
is dead,' trying how it would sound."

" Hush—hush !" he says, unutterably
pained ; then, after a little silence, " Lenore" (speaking with a shaking voice and
quivering features), " even if you are right
—even if you are not to live long—why do
you make me face this frightful possibility?
But even if it is so, let me at least be able
to look back out of my desolation, and
think, that though God was in a hurry to
part us, yet that for a short time—after
long and weary waiting—you were my
very own—belonging to me—called by my
name."

" If I am to die," she says, harshly,
"what does it matter what name I am
called by ?—what name is cut on my grave-
stone ? Shall I lie any the easier because
you wear crape and weepers for me ?"

Again he says, " Hush ! hush !"

" You are unwise to wish that I were

well," she says presently, with a sort of
pitying smile, "it is against your own interest.   I am quite fond of you now—
quite ! I like to feel your hand coolly
clasping mine ; I like to send you on messages ; you are so zealous and so speedy.
I like to see your handsome sorrowful face
come in at the door."

Again he bends his head over her hand,
to hide his dumb agony.

" If you had not been here I should have
sadly felt the want of some one to cry over
me," she continues, mournfully smiling ;
" nobody else would have done it, certainly.
I do not blame them ; I never cried over
anybody else, or was at all pitiful or sympa-
thetic in my day.   I reap my own sowing,
but still it is pleasanter as it is."

He is kissing her hands over and over
again, but he makes no rejoinder.

" But yet," she pursues gravely, " I have
a misgiving that if I grew strong and well

again I should have as little relish for your
society as ever ; I should shrink from your
touch, and fly at the distant sound of your
voice, as I did in the old days of our engagement.   Do not look miserable ; my
affection for you will never be put to that
test—only say nothing more about my being your wife ; I wish for that as little as
ever.   I love you as a child loves its nurse,
not as a woman loves her husband."

Poor Scrope ! his last Spanish castle has
fallen into ruin : by her cold and friendly
words she has torn into tatters the airy fabric
of his last poor dream.

" I was wrong," he says, after a pause, in
a strangled voice, " selfish, as I always am.
I will be—be—content."

A long, long silence.   Outside, the cheery
footsteps of guests in the hotel running
down stairs, in preparation for some pleasant expedition ; loud and happy voices,
calling to one another.   Lenore lies back

with closed eyes, exhausted by the previous conversation, and yet it is she that resumes it.

" How long do they give me ?" she asks, faintly, but calmly; " if you are truly my friend, you will tell me—No ? Well, then I must remain in my ignorance."

Another pause; the gay picnic party have packed themselves into their carriage; with a noise of wheels and bells they are off.

" Before you go," says Lenore, again speaking, " I have one more thing to say to you; it will pain you sharply, but that is nothing new, is it? you will writhe and shudder, as I have already seen you do two or three times to-day—well—I cannot help it—you are the only person I can speak to about it; if I were to broach the subject to Jemima she would put her fingers in her ears, and run out of the room."

" What is it ?" he asks indistinctly.

"When—it is—all over," she says, very slowly, but with composure, "when I am ——*gone*, do not let them take me back to England; was not it Chateaubriand who said that there was something revolting to him in the idea of a dead person on a journey ?—well—I agree with him. Make them bury me here—in the little mountain graveyard, where you and I sat on that Sunday evening, when first you came— are you listening ?—will you promise ?"

"I promise," he answers, unsteadily.

"How grand it was !" she says, leaning back, with closed eyes, and smiling dreamily. "I see them now— all those great peaks cutting the pale green sky with their jagged teeth—now that I am to leave the world so soon, I wish it were uglier; perhaps it would be easier to go—oh, my God !" (opening her eyes, and clasping her hands together in utter bitterness of spirit), "I do love this very world—just as it is—

other people find fault with it, but I do not
—I love it—I love it—oh, why may not I
stay a little in it ?"

       *   *   *   *   *   *

"Bury me under the west wall," she
says, "beneath the catchfly and the blown
dandelions !"

CHAPTER X.

WHAT JEMIMA SAYS.

ET another month has smoothly slidden past, and we are here still. We know not how much longer we may have to bide here; but, alas! we do know that when we go we shall not all go ; but that one of us, whether we will it or not, must stay behind. One of us God has called, saying to her, both in the dark night and in the broad blue noon, "Come!" and to that strong bidding there can be said no "Nay." This is an invitation to which we cannot say, "I will

not," or " I will." Bidden, one must go.
Thus our Lenore is going. We say so
now, and so it is. At first, we did not
breathe it even to ourselves ; then, after a
while, each whispered it low to her own
sad heart : *now*, we say it aloud to one
another.

We have been here ten weeks ; the
summer, that we found in its first cool
youth, has now assumed the hot gravity of
its August ripeness. We have outlived
many lovely dynasties of the flowers ; have
seen them arise and prosper, and then
sweetly die. Oh ! flowers, give us a
lesson ; teach us your way of dying, your
gentle, unregretting extinction. *Our* death
is a cruel fellow ; he is not content to take
us with a kindly mildness. Did he but
stretch out a friendly hand to us, some
among us would not be over loth to put
ours in it, and go away with him whither
he list. But he comes with his eyeless,

ash-grey skull-face ; with his racks and his
scourges ; can he blame us that we shrink
and shiver away from him ?   Lenore has
been looking him steadily in the face now,
for a long time past, but still she shivers,
still she pales, at the sound of his nearing
feet.   Lenore is amongst those who go,
knowing it.   Some depart smiling ; igno-
rantly babbling of fond home trifles, with
eyes still fixed on earth's dear sunshiny
hills and plains.   Overhead in the flood
are they plunged, or ever they know that
they are within sight of its bank.   But
Lenore knows.   I am uncertain whether
we should ever have had the heart to tell
her ; whether we should not have let her
slip into the next world, without being
aware of it.   For myself, I think it the
kinder plan ; I think that to one whom
God has summoned, *himself* will reveal it
in meet time, without the intervention of
any harsh human voice, saying roughly,

" You will die." But, as you know, an
accident has revealed it to Lenore. Sometimes she forgets it for a moment ; sometimes the conquered spirit of youth reas-
serts itself ; sometimes she talks gaily of
what she will do next year ; sometimes she
rives our hearts by making plans for the
winter, whose snows she will never feel, for
the new distant spring, whose flowers will
open upon her grave. But it is only for a
little while that the beautiful illusion lives ;
always it vanishes, as the cold dew vanishes
from the fine fresh mountain grass.

It is a fearfully hot day, softly overcast ;
the keen mountain air, cool and crisp,
which so rarely fails from these high places,
has gone to draw new sharpness from the
snows, and left us gasping. A silent day,
but for the loud rumblings of the thunder
in the great grand hills.

Sylvia sits in her bedroom, crying over
the last volume of a Tauchnitz novel, be-

nevolently lent her by Mrs. Scrope, which makes her hotter still. Lenore lies, with heavy eyelids drooped over sunk eyes, on the sofa in our sitting-room; it has been transformed, as much as possible, into the likeness of a couch, and drawn up close to the window, to catch any stray little travelling breeze. Breathing is always difficult to Lenore now, but to-day specially so. I am sitting beside her, fanning her. She expressed a while ago a sudden longing for lemonade, as a nice cool drink. I asked Kolb to make me some, as it is a beverage which does not grow ready made in these parts. Kolb's lemonade is produced by pouring hot water on lemons; five minutes ago it entered *boiling*. I have been pouring the whole stock of water contained in my bedroom's tiny ewer and bottle into a washhand basin, and causing the lemonade jug to stand in it, in the forlorn hope of cooling it through the agency of this half-pint of tepid water. Now I have returned to Lenore, and am fanning her again. The languid flies come and march about upon her outflung arms, with their little tickling, maddening legs, and when I strike out wildly and indignantly at them, with a little self-conscious buzz they fly away and elude me. With my resentful eyes I have followed one to the wall, where he stands twisting his hind legs together. Then my sad gaze returns to the place where it has dwelt all morning—Lenore's sunken, weary, pained face; the face that might as well be any one else's, for all resemblance that it bears to hers—hers, our beauty! Oh, bad, cruel Death! Why cannot you take us all at once, without first stealing beauty and grace and harmony? Do you care to hold nothing but disfigurement and decay in your frosty arms! I am sorrowfully pondering on the probability of her passing to-day—half wishing it, and yet half grudging—when her eyes slowly unclose, and she speaks.

"You fan me badly," she says, feebly and complainingly ; "so irregularly, and inter- mittingly—not half so well as Charlie does. Send him."

"But, my dear," I say, gently remon- strating, "you always *will* talk to him, you know, and you are not up to it."

"I *mean* to talk to him," she says, with a pitiful shadow of her old resolute wilful- ness. "I have something to say to him— something I *must* say to him—a favour to ask of him."

"A favour ?"

"Yes," she answers petulantly, "a favour ; but it is nothing to you ; it is not you that I am going to ask—send him."

So I obey. I find him sitting in his own room, his hands thrust into his tossed bright hair, and his eyes, red with watching and weeping, idly fixed on the cruel calm of the unfeeling smiling hills. "She has sent for you," I say, entering listlessly. "She says you fan her so much better than I do. She has also something to say to you, a favour to ask—a *favour*—what can it be?" I end, a little inquisitively. He does not pay any heed to my curiosity; he is already in the passage when I call him back. ".Stay," I say; "before you go, bathe your eyes and try to smile; you know, poor soul, she—she likes us to look cheerful."

CHAPTER XI.

WHAT THE AUTHOR SAYS.

" HOW long you have been!" she says, querulously. "I thought you were never coming. You might have made a little haste."

" I will be quicker next time, darling," he answers, kneeling down gently beside her, and speaking firmly and cheerfully.

" Fan me," she says, panting; " fan me strongly and regularly."

She lies back exhausted, and he hears her mutter, " At least, wherever I go, I shall have breath."

Utter silence for five minutes, save for

the gentle noise made by the winnowing of the fan.

" Lift me," she says, stretching out her arms to him.   " Lying down I gasp."

He lifts her with delicate care, and her dying head droops in sisterly abandonment on his kind shoulder.

" Dear old fellow," she says faintly ; " kind old brother."

Yet another pause ; no sustained conversation is possible.

" I am going very fast, Charlie."

" Yes, darling."

" I was always one to do things quickly, if I did them at all — I was never a dawdle."

No answer.

" You will get away before the season is over, after all."

" Oh, love, hush !"

" You would do something to oblige me, would not you, Charlie ?"

" Anything possible, beloved."

" But supposing it were impossible ?"

" Still I would do it."

" That is right," she answers, with a sigh of relief.

" I am glad."

Then she is again silent for a long time. The thunder still grumbles deeply in the hot heart of the hills, and the flies still walk about torpidly upon her white wrapper.

" You know all the old story—about Paul," she says presently, with a little excitement in her faint and hollow voice.

" Yes, I know it."

" You know the reason why I have borrowed the advertisement sheet of your *Times* every day ?"

" I—I have guessed it."

" I have daily looked carefully through the marriages," she says, with a sort of feeble eagerness, " but I have never seen *his.*"

" Neither have I."

A long and painful fit of coughing inter-
venes.

" Tell me the rest to-morrow," he says,
gently bending over her.   She smiles
slightly.

" It is all very well for *you* to talk—*you*
who are rich in to-morrows.   How do I
know that I have one ?"

Again he fans her, trying to coax the
cool little waves of air to her hot and parted
lips.

" He said it—was—to be *immediately*,"
she murmurs after a pause ; "since it has
not been yet—perhaps—it will never be."

" Perhaps."

" Very likely it is broken off," she says,
a ray of pleasure lighting up her face.   " I
never told you so before—but—between
ourselves—I do not think—he was very
eager about it.   No doubt it is broken off."

" No doubt."

She has taken his hand, and is stroking it with a sort of patronising caressingness.

" Kind, good, patient Charlie !" she says softly. " Whose errands will you run on when I am gone ?"

No answer.

" I have *one* more errand to send you on," she continues, with feeble eagerness ; " longer, disagreeabler, more difficult than any of the others. Will you run on it too ?"

" Oh, beloved, try me !"

" There is at least one advantage in being in a dying state," she says by-and-by, gravely and solemnly ; "as long as I was well I could not send for him—could not ask him to come back to me—could not move a finger to bring him—all the advances must have come from *him*. But now—*now* —I may send for whom I please, and no one will call me unmaidenly, will they ?"

" No one," he answers steadily, though

his face is drawn with the pain of finding that still, in these last hours, he is second, always second. She is looking earnestly at him ; her large grey eyes—unnaturally, unbecomingly large now—are reading his countenance like an open book.

" It hurts you," she says calmly ; " well, I have always hurt you. I suppose you like it, or you would not have stayed with me, but would have gone, as Paul did. Well, have I made you understand ? I wish to send for him."

For a second he turns away his head, and gathers his strength together ; then he says, kindly and gently :

" Do you wish me to write or telegraph ?"

" I wish neither," she answers, with a little impatience; " do you think that *that* is my errand ? That would not be a very hard one, just to walk down to the post-office; I might charge even Sylvia with that. Listen ; of course you need not do it unless you wish ; of course I cannot *make* you. I wish to make sure. I wish you to *go and fetch him.*"

He gives an involuntary start of utter pain and anguish.

" And leave *you*, oh my darling ?"

" And leave me," she echoes pettishly; "what good do you do me ? What good does any one do me ? Can you give me breath or sleep ?"

He rises and walks to the window. The evening draws on, and the thunder is dumb. He looks out on the great mountains—lilac while the sun is setting, grey when he is gone—the mountains whose playfellows the swift snow-storms are, and about whose necks the clouds wreathe their wet white arms ; looks at the deep torrent courses that furrow their sides, and at the straight dark pines, which the winter strips not, and to whom lavish spring, with her gentian wreath and her lap full of flowered grasses, brings no embellishment ; looks at them all, without seeing them. Then he comes back to the couch side, and says :

" I will go."

" You think he will not come ?" she says looking wistfully at him. " I see it in your face, but I know better ; if you had seen him at Bergun, you would have thought differently. Yes " (with a little shining smile), " he will come !"

" There is no doubt of it," he replies quietly.

" Even if he is married he will come," she says, still smiling ; " his wife will spare him for these few days, and, if she hesitates, you may tell her that, whatever I was once, I am not a person to be jealous of now."

Silence.

" You will set off to-morrow morning *early*," she says feverishly. " I am afraid it is too late to-day. You know his address ? Oh yes, of course ; you have been there ?"

" Yes."

"And you will *certainly* bring him— *certainly* ?"

" Yes."

She closes her eyes with a long sigh of relief. She lies so still that he is uncertain whether she sleeps, but, after a time, she opens them again.

" You wonder why I wish so much to see him again," she says slowly; "when he does not wish to see me ; you think it is *love.* No, it is not. When one is sick as I am one is past love ; only all the night through his face *vexes* me. I am worried with it; it never leaves me ; I torment myself trying to recall every line of it. I *must* see whether I have remembered it right : it has been with me every moment in this world. I must take it distinct and clear with me into the next."

CHAPTER XII.

"Lilies for a bridal bed;
  Roses for a matron's head;
  Violets for a maiden dead."

WHAT JEMIMA SAYS.

CHARLIE is gone. Very early to-day he set off. I stood by him on the steps, in the cool of the young and shining morning, as he prepared to step into the carriage which was to take him up and down the long steep mountain passes to Chur.

"Keep her till I come back," he said, wringing my hand with unknowing violence.

" If I come back to find her gone, I shall never forgive you—never. Promise !"

" How can I promise ?" I said, sorrowfully. " Have I life and death in my hand? How can I hinder her going ?"

So he is gone, and we are waiting— waiting with strained ears and hot eyes— to see which will win the race to Lenore's side, Death or Paul. Lenore herself fights with all her strength—alas, how little !— with a strength not her own—on Paul's side. She *refuses* to die. For more than a week past she has turned with loathing from every species of nourishment ; now she demands it greedily. She will not speak—will not utter a word—for fear of wasting the little breath that remains to her. People are very kind ; every hour of the day solicitous faces meet us on the landing-place, with pitying gestures and expressions of sympathy. Guests in the hotel tread softly, and scold their children when they hear them whooping and noisily tumbling, with the utter unfeelingness of childhood, down the slight stairs and along the thin-walled passages.

*   *   *   *   *

And now all the days between Scrope's going and his expected backcoming have rolled away. Before he went we calculated accurately together distances and times ; this is the day on which he engaged to return. Lenore is still here—still fighting—disputing her life, inch by inch, hand to hand, with the all-victor.

" He will come to-day," she has said, speaking for the first time for many hours —speaking confidently. " It is my lucky day ; something tells me so."

I have drawn the scant window-curtain and thrown wide the window, and looked out on the unutterable majesty of the morning hills.

" I *will not* die to-day !" she says, clenching her feeble hand. "I have some life left in me yet—more than you think. It would be too cruel to go before he came ; he would be so disappointed." I turn and gaze mournfully at her. Her voice is stronger, and the inward excitement of her soul has sent a last little flame of colour to her cheeks. "Let us be ready for him," she says, with a tender smile. "Take away all those physic bottles—everything that looks like sickness. Make the room pretty ; gather plenty of flowers."

So I obey her. All about the room, following her directions, I place the gay sweet flowers. Oh, wonderful, lovely flowers! whence do you steal your tender stains ? Is it from the brown earth or the colourless wind ? Later on, as the day draws towards noon, she expresses a wish to be dressed. I remonstrate gently, fearing the exhaustion consequent on so unwonted an exertion ; but she is resolute.

" I shall wish so few things any more,"
she says, simply and pleadingly ; " you
may as well let me have my way." Thus
I tearfully consent. " The old blue gown,"
she says, with an eager smile ; " Louise
will find it among my things. It is the
only one among my clothes that he ever
praised. He never was one to notice
clothes, but he liked that. Only the last
time I saw him he was talking of it."

So, with many pauses, slowly and
mournfully, with sorrowful faces, as if we
were already dressing her for her grave, we
dress her in the old blue gown. Alas ! it
is pitifully large for her. But she is not
yet satisfied. In spite of pain, in spite of
utter prostration, she must also have her
hair dressed—her long bright hair—the
one thing that remains to her.

" Plait it round and round my head,"
she says, looking with feverish entreaty
into my sad face. " Take great pains.

Put no *frisettes* — nothing artificial; he does not like it; but yet let it be becoming."

Becoming! at such a time! Oh, God! Amazed I look at her, and a half doubt enters my mind that I have been allotting her too short a span of further life. Her voice sounds certainly stronger, and there is a ray of living animation in her great sunken eyes. Towards evening she grows very restless, and I hear her murmur to herself, " He must make haste—make haste. The road is long and steep—so many sharp turns and twists. I hope the horses are sure-footed. But it is only for *once;* he might make 'haste." She is as one running a hard race that is nearing the · goal, but hears his rival's feet close upon his track, and strains every tense nerve in the effort and agony of attainment. Will she attain her goal? It is the question that, as day droops into night, makes us all ever more and more breathless. She speaks little with her faint lips, but with her hunted piteous eyes she *entreats* us to keep her. I cannot bear those eyes.

The light is gone, and the candles are lit. " Let me read to you a little," I say, softly, in a tear-strangled voice.

" Yes," she answers; " yes; if you will —if you like."

But she is not listening. I sit down with the Bible upon my knees. I can hardly see the page for tears. I scarcely know where I turn. I begin at the words of godlike consolation that fit any grief; that come never amiss : " Come unto me all ye that labour and are heavy laden." They open the fount of my own sorrow, that requires but a touch to unclose it. " Are you listening ?" I ask, gently, trying to scan her face across the candle's feeble flame.

" Yes," she answers, with a sort of hurry ;
" yes—to be sure—I am listening ! — but
read lower ; one cannot hear any little
noise outside when you read so loud."

Sighing, I lay down the book, and walking to the window look out—look out at the
little quarter moon, and the travelling stars
—the sky, that speaks of sleep and unutterable quietness—the dark mountain bulks,
with flashes of silver on their giant flanks—
the narrow street, with the lights from the
hotel playing on the little houses opposite
—the small white cross gleaming in the
moonlight—the solitary pacer down the
tongueless street—the solemn glacier river
that saith nothing light, but singeth ever
the same plain, hoarse song.

" After all—I shall have to go !" she
says, with a low wail. " I cannot wait—I
cannot. Oh, Paul ! you might have hur-
ried !"

I have thrust my head as far out of the

window as it will go. I am listening. At
first, nothing but the river—nothing! Oh,
river! I hate you; be silent for once.
Then a little noise mixes with it—so small
and uncertain that one cannot positively
say at first that it is not a part of the
stream's roar; then it separates itself—
grows distinct—nears. I turn to the bed,
with an unspeakable weight lifted from my
heart. "He is coming!" I say, with a
smile; but already she has heard. Could
I expect my ears to be keener than hers?
Even in death she looks very joyful. As
the carriage noisily rolls up towards the
hotel I turn with the intention of going
down to meet the travellers; but she stops
me.

"Stay!" she says, stretching out her
hand eagerly. "Do not go! I forbid
you! I will have the first look!"

So we remain in absolute silence for two
enormous minutes; then the sound of a

step running quickly and lightly up the stairs—*a* step—surely there is only *one !* The door opens, and Charlie enters, haggard, travel-stained, and *alone.* She does not even look at him ; her eyes are staring with an awful eager intentness at the door behind him ; but no one follows, nor does he leave it open, as if expecting to be followed. On the contrary, he closes it behind him.

" Great God !" I say, running up to him, half out of my wits with excitement, " What is this ? You have come without him ? You have not brought him ?"

He does not answer.

Putting me aside he goes hastily to the couch, kneels down beside it, taking her gently in his arms, and says, in a hoarse voice :

" My darling, I have broken my promise —but I could not help it ;—it was not my fault. He—he—has not come, because—

because it was his wedding-day when I got there. Oh, beloved, speak to me! Say you forgive me—you are not going without *one* word—speak—speak !"

But Lenore will never speak to him any more : her head has sunk back, with all its pretty careful plaits, on his shoulder—Lenore has

" Gone thro' the straight and dreadful pass of death."

THE END.

BILLING, PRINTER, GUILDFORD, SURREY.

BENTLEY'S FAVOURITE NOVELS.

With Illustrations. Crown 8vo. 6s. each.

Red as a Rose is She. By the Author of 'Cometh up as a Flower.'

Cometh up as a Flower. By the Author of ' Red as a Rose is She.'

Bessy Rane. By Mrs. HENRY WOOD.

Verner's Pride. By Mrs. HENRY WOOD.

Roland Yorke. By Mrs. HENRY WOOD.

Mrs. Gerald's Niece. By the Hon. Lady GEORGIANA FULLERTON.

Breezie Langton. A Story of '52 to '55. By HAWLEY SMART.

Lady Adelaide's Oath. By the Author of ' East Lynne.'

Anthony Trollope's Three Clerks.

Too Strange not to be True. By Lady GEORGIANA FULLERTON.

Quits. By the Author of ' Initials.'

East Lynne. By Mrs. HENRY WOOD.

The Channings. By the Author of ' East Lynne.'

Mrs. Halliburton's Troubles. By the same Author.

The Initials. By the Author of 'Quits,' 'At Odds,' &c.

Miss Austen's Sense and Sensibility.

——————— Emma.

——————— Pride and Prejudice.

——————— Mansfield Park.

——————— Northanger Abbey and Persuasion.

——————— Lady Susan and the Watsons.

RICHARD BENTLEY AND SON, New Burlington Street.